For my best friends

J, H, A, & A

My ship, my anchor, and the stars which guide me home.

To learn more about *Screaming in the Silence*, visit:

www.worldmakermedia.com/screaming

Chapter 1

I felt the vibration before I realized what it was. I saw the pitch black interior before I realized where I was. And I felt a body, still warm, lying next to me before I remembered who she was. I almost gagged at the strong smell of blood. Something thick and crusty was smeared across my cheek and forehead. I scratched my fingernails over it and it crumbled away in flakes.

I felt the car gain speed and the body rolled on top of me. Was it Julie? I pushed it away with a sob, wondering if she was still alive, hoping she was still alive.

Then, before I could brace myself, I was thrown towards the front of the truck. The back opened and a dim light flooded in.

It was Julie. Moonlight lit her blood soaked hair. The gaping wound in her skull made her almost unrecognizable. Her eyes and mouth were open in horrific panic and her neck bone jutted against the skin like a needle attempting to push through fabric. Scrambling, I pushed away from her, closed my eyes as I hung my torso out of the car, and vomited onto the ground below me. I inhaled deeply, appreciating the crisp ocean air.

With my head dizzy from confusion and nausea, I slowly raised my eyes to view a face. A tall, glaring man stood over me with the look of a predator eyeing its prey. The car shook again and two more faces appeared.

"What the fuck is this? You said they were both dead." The face on the right spoke, its expression scared and confused.

"I thought they were," the tall man's lips moved slowly. He was thinking as he spoke.

"What are we supposed to do now, Ray?" The man on the right had turned his attention away from me, making it difficult to determine what he was saying.

"Kill her." There was no mistaking what he had said.

I shook my head in panic. I looked back to the man on the right, perhaps he would disagree with Ray. His eyes returned to me without a trace of remorse for what he was about to do.

A third man who I hadn't noticed before stood on the left. He moved quickly, grabbing me by the shoulders and throwing me from the car. Excruciating pain shot up my body as I was dragged across the bumper and then over the rough ground. My clothes ripped and I kicked my legs furiously, trying to find my footing so I could stand. As soon as I was on my feet, I felt a hard body press against my back, holding me up and pinning my arms in front of my chest, with one strong hand around my wrists. His other hand fingered the material of my shirt, flipping the ends of my hair, and pointing to my shoes. I couldn't see the man who was holding me. His grip was firm yet his rough fingers held me gently. Ray and the other man stared at us, their faces brightening like I was a prize.

"The basement? It could work." Ray nodded at the man behind me before his eyes locked onto mine.

"What's your name?"

A scene flashed through my mind. We were standing by the side of the road, our thumbs up, hoping to find our way back to a city of reasonable size. The beach had been pleasant during the day, but now the wind was picking up and the area between the road and cliff's edge offered no protection. It was becoming dark outside so she stepped in front of me, turning to explain that her white shirt would be more visible than my dark blue one. The car came around the bend, completely out of control, and the last thing I remembered was being thrown over the hood of the car as her head smacked the windshield.

Julie. Her name was Julie.

Ray waved his hands in front of me.

"What is your name?" He repeated his question. They hadn't realized.

The wind bit at my nose and chin and I couldn't keep my hair from flying between us. Ray didn't seem to mind and moved within inches of my face. The arms behind me hugged tighter.

"What. Is. Your. Name."

I felt warm breath on my ear and turned my eyes from Ray. The man holding me had his lips close to my face and he was saying something that I couldn't decipher from the angle.

Fingers harshly grabbed my chin and turned my face.

"Answer me!"

I could feel the vibrations from his yell. His breath smelled of rum. I managed to free one of my hands.

R-A-L-E-I-G-H. I spelled my name, knowing they wouldn't understand.

"What the hell was that?" Ray started laughing and he turned back to the smaller man, who stood by the car.

"Sign language?" Ray's attention suddenly returned to me. I took a deep breath and brought my free hand to the side of my face. My fingers went to my ear, tapping lightly as I shook my head.

"Shit. She's deaf," he said to the man behind me.

He spun me around and I came face to face with brilliant green eyes. His dark eyebrows furrowed beneath black hair, which hung to his brows and swept across his forehead. His cheekbones were high and chiseled, his jaw square and strong.

"Can you read lips?"

I nodded slowly.

His lips twitched into a sly and sordid smile.

"Can you speak?"

I didn't answer at first, not sure if I wanted them to know the truth. Maybe it would be easier if they didn't know everything I was capable of. So I shook my head, swallowed my answer in my throat, and lied. Silence hadn't scared me in this way since I was six years old.

He still held my shoulders in his strong hands. He squeezed me harder and I thought for a moment he was trying to reassure me. However, the look on this man's face told me otherwise. This gesture was one of domination and it terrified me.

Suddenly and without warning, I was thrown over his shoulder, my body hanging down his back like a sack of potatoes. I nearly vomited again from the pain in my chest but I managed to look under his arm to see the smaller man pull Julie from the car, her head and arms bouncing as she fell from the trunk. With Ray's help, he pulled her by the feet to the cliff's edge. I didn't want to think about what was going to happen to her body. With a final push she was rolled out of sight and into the violent waves below.

As I was thrown back into the trunk, I clung to the shirt of the man with the green eyes. I struggled to get out of the trunk, grabbing his plaid flannel shirt. His hands pinned my shoulders to the carpeted floor.

"Stop. You'll hurt yourself."

The door closed on top of me and my silent world went black. My screaming did nothing but make my throat burn. If a tree falls in the forest when no one is around to hear it, does it still make a sound? If I scream in the silence, will anyone be around to hear it?

Chapter 2

My screaming ceased to bring me comfort a few turns into the drive. I relaxed onto my back, the most comfortable position I could find considering how badly bruised and beaten I was. Large tears fell from my eyes and mixed with the blood on my face. I wanted to sleep, I wanted to dream, I wanted to be pulled from this nightmare but even with my eyes closed, sleep alluded me.

"Hi, I'm Julie."

"I'm Raleigh. Very nice to meet you."

The look she gave me was a curious one. I was used to this reaction and it didn't faze me any longer. At a younger age, it had hurt and I had been ashamed of my voice. Ashamed enough that I had wanted to remain silent. But I learned to move past it. I learned that I had quite a bit to say and even though I couldn't hear it, even though it sounded strange to others, my voice was worth the hassle of explaining my condition.

"Where are you from?"

"Delaware."

"Oh. I didn't recognize your accent."

I smiled at her. "I'm deaf. There's no accent."

Her face reddened and she looked apologetic. "Shit. Now I feel bad."

But I shook my head. "Don't worry about it. It happens."

She nodded. "So if you're from Delaware, what are you doing all the way down here?"

"Sightseeing."

"Right. Sightseeing at a trucker stop in Tennessee?"

"I'm trying to get to the coast," I explained. "I got a ride all the way from Indiana."

"No shit! That far? How long did you have to wait for that one?"

"A few days." I smiled at her. I liked this girl. It had been a while since I had spoken with a female my own age.

"Which beach are you trying to make it to?" She picked up her bag from the ground and slung it over her shoulder.

"It doesn't really matter, I guess. Just one with an ocean."

"Well, I'm on my way to North Carolina if you'd like to tag along. I could sure use the company. These truckers aren't the best conversationalists."

I smiled and nodded, agreeing completely. Julie was the first female hitcher I had met and I was in desperate need of a friend. The road from Delaware had been lonely and even though I had the company of whoever stopped to pick me up, I knew our relationship would be short lived.

"Alright, then! Let's go find us a ride! Two pretty girls like us should have no problem getting picked up." *She smiled at me and extended her hand. I stood up from the curb where I was sitting and followed her to the first driver in a long line of waiting trucks, eager to see where this new relationship would take me.*

My breath became heavy as I felt the car roll to a stop. Part of me wanted the three men to forget about me and leave me in the trunk. The other part was dying to stand up and stretch my sore arms and legs. I knew I needed to see a doctor. At least one of my ribs was broken and I wasn't sure how deep the cuts on my face and torso were. But a doctor was out of the question and even if I had been naive enough to ask for one, I knew I would be laughed at.

The trunk popped open and I blinked at the light. We must have driven all night and into the morning because the sun was high in the sky. As my eyes adjusted, I saw the smallest of the three men speaking to me. More like yelling at me.

"Get out!" I could tell he was screaming from the muscles chorded in his neck.

I sat up and looked around warily, not expecting to recognize where I was but hoping for a miracle. Pine trees surrounded us in every direction. An overrun dirt road forked up a hill. A quaint and unimposing house with yellow trim and a brick façade sat in between the trees.

I climbed out of the car and winced at the pain in my ribs. The small man closed his pudgy fingers around my arms and led me to the front door, which had been left open by Ray and the man with the green eyes. The inside of this house did not do justice to the outside. The windows were all open yet there was a heavy, stale smell in the air. The carpets were dirty and ripped from the floor near the walls. The wallpaper was stained and peeling.

The two men were already seated at a table, one of the few pieces of furniture in the house, pouring out the contents of my bag. Julie's bag sat on the floor next to them.

There, mere feet from me, being carelessly thrown about, were the entire contents of my life. Everything I owned and all I could carry with me. Clothes, underwear, toothbrush, expensive make-up - I couldn't leave my vanity behind - and my wallet. It contained my only identification.

Ray found the wallet and grabbed it, opening the leather pouch and eyeing what was inside.

"Raleigh Anne Winters from Dover, Delaware. Never heard of it." I watched him throw my ID aside and continue going through my wallet. I felt violated. What gave him the right?

"Three hundred and fifty-eight bucks...not bad." Ray handed the money to the man with the green eyes. He glanced at me suspiciously.

"Any credit cards?" he asked.

"Four."

My stare returned to his green eyes. He stood up and walked toward me, leaving the cash on the table. "Give her to me."

The small man handed me over as Ray watched.

"Where are you taking her?"

His grip was just as strong as it had been last night. He turned to face his friend at the table and said something I couldn't see. Ray nodded and returned to my bag. I found myself pulled from the room and up the stairs. Horrifying scenarios raced through my head. I struggled against him, tripping and scraping my shins on the splintered stairs. I could only imagine what he was going to do to me and I wasn't ready for any of it. I pulled against his hand, pushed his arm away with all my strength but nothing helped and I was too sore to fight for long.

At the top of the stairs, he pushed me into the bathroom and pinned me against a wall.

His face hovered inches from me.

"Look, you may not be able to hear me, but I don't believe for a minute that you can't speak. Everything about you from your designer jeans to the four credit cards in your wallet screams Daddy's money and higher education so if you want to keep up the act, that's fine. Just know that I'm not letting you out of my sights. You aren't going to fuck this up for me."

I stared at him, more of a glare, really, and waited for him to say something else. This man was perceptive and even if he didn't know who I was or why I had been on the side of the road, he knew my type: spoiled brat from up North with too many advantages and not enough ambition. He glared back, challenging me to speak but when I didn't, he released my shoulders and took a few steps back, lowering the lid to the toilet and sitting down.

"Shower," he commanded and pointed to the curtain. "You look like shit."

I looked away from him and glanced in the mirror. The girl staring back at me was not someone I recognized. Her once blonde hair now appeared brown from all of the blood and dirt. Her grey eyes were red and swollen and blood was smeared from her forehead to her neck and caked around her nose. Her lips were cracked. I had to look away as tears welled up behind my lids.

The man with the green eyes stood up from his seat and pulled back the dingy and stained shower curtain, pointing for me to climb in. I shook my head. He was crazy if he thought I was going to get undressed with him still in the room. But he grabbed my hand and pulled me toward the tub. It was stained with mold and rust. I had used cleaner ones at the truck stops I had been through in the past few months.

I looked up at him and pointed toward the door. A warm shower would feel good right now but not with him watching.

"I'm not leaving." His stern face glanced to the window above the sink and I finally understood his reasoning. If he knew how much pain I was in, he would certainly have realized that jumping from a second story window was out of the question.

"You can either shower with or without my help. But you need to." His face softened and he reached for my arm. "It will be good for you."

I pushed his arm away and signed for him to fuck off before I stepped out of my sandals.

His fingers gripped my cheeks and he jerked my head up to look at him. "Fuck you, too."

I stepped back in surprise. He had understood?

His lips crept over his teeth as he smiled at me. "You're not the only one with secrets."

I flashed a mockingly sweet smile, tears streaming from my eyes. He laughed and released my face, pointing again to the shower and grabbing a towel from the shelf above my head. I slowly undid the buttons on my jeans, not wanting to bend over to pull them down because I knew how badly it would hurt. I managed to wiggle them down my hips and step out of them. He returned to his seat on the toilet and stared at me with a concerned expression. It angered me but I looked away, not wanting him to know that his presence bothered me.

I tugged at the bottom of my shirt and attempted to lift it over my head but the pain in my chest was too much and I cried out as my shirt fell back into place. I held my eyes shut until the throbbing lessened, fresh tears of pain and embarrassment falling onto my cheeks. The man was standing in front of me when my eyes opened and I jumped, startled he could move so quickly.

"Sorry," his mouth twitched at the corners like he wanted to smile. "Let me help you. Arms up."

I hesitated but obeyed and he carefully pulled my blood stained shirt from my body. The shirt was matted to my skin and I winced as it tore the wounds. I sighed in relief once it was over my head. He threw the shirt on the floor next to the remnants of my jeans and bent over the tub to turn on the water. I watched him carefully, unsure of what to think. Was he really trying to help me or did he have ulterior motives? It had been him, after all, who had convinced Ray to spare my life. What did he want with me?

I put all of these questions aside as the steam started to fill the room, soothing my aching muscles. The man with the green eyes stood up once the temperature was to his liking and looked at me.

"Thank you," I said, barely using my voice at all.

He smiled at me as if he had won a contest. "You're welcome, Raleigh."

"What's your name?" I asked, no longer caring that I was having this conversation in my underwear.

He lifted one large hand and spelled it out for me. *K-A-D-E-N.*

I nodded and turned away from him, slipping out of my panties and bra before stepping into the shower.

Chapter 3

I stayed in the shower until the hot water ran out. The blood washed from my body to reveal dark bruises but only minor lacerations. I pressed lightly around my ribs but couldn't feel anything out of place, although the pain was agonizing. Turning off the water, I peaked around the curtain to see Kaden holding a towel, his head turned away from me. I took it and pulled it around my torso, unable to wrap it too tightly, then climbed out. The steam still filled the room. Kaden's face was damp, his hair pushed out of his eyes, spiking to the sides and looking perfectly disheveled. His shirt stuck to his chest, his broad shoulders framing the muscles underneath.

I shouldn't have been staring; I shouldn't have given him a second thought. He had kidnapped me, taken away my life and identity with one hit of his car and one split decision. I knew he was no better than the men downstairs who didn't have half a care for the woman they had in their upstairs bathroom. But I needed something to hold on to. Some shred of hope that I would survive whatever they had planned for me.

Kaden's bright green eyes danced over my face and body, showing curiosity but no emotion. "You're blonde." I couldn't tell if he was asking a question or making a statement.

"You're perceptive."

"Was that sarcasm or a compliment?"

"I'll call it an honest remark."

Kaden's eyes laughed at me but his lips pulled into a frown. "Get dressed."

He handed me a clean pair of jeans, now my only pair, some cotton panties and a t-shirt, presumably one of his or possibly Ray's judging by the size.

"I want my own clothes."

Kaden didn't say anything, just crossed his arms and stared at me.

Give me my clothes, I signed to him.

"Sorry, darling. No can do. Get dressed."

I turned away, setting my jeans and shirt on the edge of the sink and picking up the underwear. I raised one foot slowly, careful not to let the towel drop or crush my ribs, and slipped the panties up to my ankle. But my lack of food and water had left me shaky and standing on one leg quickly caused me to lose my balance. I caught myself on the sink, cringing and gasping in pain.

As soon as I stood up and started to make my second attempt, Kaden was standing in front of me.

"Do I have to do everything for you?"

"I'm not asking you to do a damn thing."

"Yah, well, if I didn't you'd still be struggling to make it up the stairs."

Because there are so many other places you should be right now, I signed.

"If you have something to say then you should just say it," Kaden told me as he grabbed my hands.

I glared at him but eventually shook my head. I had nothing to say to him.

"I thought so." He pushed my hands aside and then knelt down by my feet, stretching the underwear out so I could step in.

I closed my eyes and instinctively clenched my thighs together. I felt his fingers run up my calves and over my knees, flames licking my skin in their wake. When they got to my thighs, I couldn't allow them to continue. I grabbed the cotton fabric and tugged it from his fingers. His hands seized my wrists and squeezed hard enough for me to give up the fight with the panties and jerk my arms away from his grasp. My underwear, along with my towel, fell to the ground and I inhaled deeply as my vulnerability was exposed.

Kaden stood up slowly, his green eyes taking their time to examine my naked body. His face was close to mine when he finally spoke. "Well, well, you really have nothing to hide now, do you?" His fingers twirled my damp hair and I trembled as he placed the curl on my naked shoulder, the back of his hand grazing the top of my breast.

"Now don't fight this time and it will be over quickly."

I looked past him, blinking away the tears. He dropped to his knees again and I felt the underwear being pulled up from my ankles and his fingers wrapping around my thin bones. His breath was warm on the damp skin of my inner thigh and he made no attempt to conceal what he was doing. His hands worked their way up the back of my calves, lifting the panties. I felt a jolt of arousal deep within me. This should not be happening! My head screamed at me to fight him off, not allow him to touch me this way. But my body was waiting to see where he would go next, waiting to see what he would try.

I kept as still as I possibly could, my breath coming in shallow pants. Cool tears rolled down my cheeks and heat rose from my legs where Kaden touched me. Why couldn't this be over? Why was he torturing me this way? Apparently it wasn't enough to nearly kill me and then capture me, before bringing me to this sordid house. Now I had to be humiliated.

Kaden's fingers grazed the back of my thighs. I looked down to see his lips pressed firmly together, his eyes focused on the task. He was so close to my naked and bruised body. His hands climbed until they reached the sensitive area just below my buttocks and then hesitated. My breath caught in my throat as I suppressed a sob and closed my eyes. His touch heightened my senses and the site of his handsome face taking such care to degrade me was overwhelming. I prayed that he would release me. Slowly and confidently, his hands spread my legs and his fingers met between them.

"Please," I whimpered as I felt one of his fingers start to press inside me. Please stop? Please continue? I'm not sure what I was begging for at the moment but I knew I couldn't take much more.

His finger remained inside of me while his other hand firmly held the back of my leg. I opened my watery eyes to see him staring up at me. He plunged deeper. I cried out, first from the shock and then a second time from the shock of the pain in my ribs as I inhaled sharply.

Before I could even attempt to recover my composure , Kaden had the elastic band of the panties around my hips. I couldn't look at him as he moved behind me and helped me with my bra, lifting my arms and maneuvering the straps over my shoulders. His hands didn't linger this time and he gently pulled the bra around my sore and blackened ribs. He set my hand on his strong shoulder so I could brace myself against something stable and then slipped on my jeans. The oversized t-shirt was last and Kaden rolled the material up so I could get my head and arms through. It hung halfway to my knees but it smelled fresh, a welcome change from the foul stench of blood and mold.

Once I was completely covered, I finally allowed myself to look at him again. Kaden stared at me and nodded, clearly proud of the job he had accomplished, as if dressing a woman was now some sort of prestigious achievement.

"Do you feel better?" Was he joking? What was there to feel better about?

"Relatively speaking."

"Come on, then. You'll want to eat something, I imagine." He sighed, an annoyed look on his face, and opened the door.

"If I'm such a burden to you, then you should let me go."

"I believe you'll be worth more than the effort it takes me to make a tuna sandwich, Blondie. But how much is yet to be determined, isn't it?" So he was after money. Money I had and I was more than willing to give it up in return for my freedom.

"If you want money, then I can get that for you. Just take me to a bank and I'll empty my account."

"Give me a number." Kaden crossed his arms in front of his chest.

I thought back to all the checks I had received for graduation, my trust fund which had kicked in on my twenty first birthday and had yet to be touched, and the bribes my father had given me for staying out of trouble.

"Twenty five," I finally answered.

"Twenty five hundred? That's not going to last me very long considering I have to split it three ways."

"Thousand. Twenty five thousand dollars."

He stopped and turned around, eyeing me with the same suspicious look he had given me downstairs. "What is a hitchhiker doing with that kind of money?"

"If I can get it for you, why would it matter?"

"Tell me, what makes you think you are in any kind of a position to be asking questions?"

I looked at the ground. I was in no position to be asking anything. But I didn't want him to know the truth. If I told him where all the money came from, he would know I was connected to people who could give him much, much, more. No, it would be better to lie, let him take what I had and leave me be.

"My parents passed away and the twenty five thousand is all that's left of my inheritance."

He walked back to me, raised my chin with his hand and, once satisfied that I was looking at him, signed his response. *L-I-A-R*

I flinched and looked away again, furious at myself for thinking the plan would work. His long fingers wrapped around my arm and started leading me out of the bathroom and back downstairs. We reached the living room where Ray and the small guy sat at the table. My possessions were still strewn about.

"What did you find out?" Ray stood up and walked over to me.

Kaden shook his head, turning it slightly toward me so I could read his lips.

"Nothing, she can't say a word."

Ray frowned and gave me a disgusted look. "So, do some of that signing shit with her."

"I will when it's worth my time."

Why was he doing this? He knew the truth yet he was keeping it from the others. My limbs began to shake as I realized he was hiding my secret for a reason. What that reason was, I couldn't imagine, I didn't want to know. I turned back to Ray.

"Well, genius, it was your plan to bring her here instead of leaving the bitch on the side of the road with her friend. You better make this inconvenience worth *my* time."

"If she won't talk, I'll get her to scream," Kaden said, his devilish smile sending shivers up my spine. Without another word, he walked me out of the room.

Chapter 4

Kaden did exactly what he said he was going to do. He sat me down in the kitchen and made me a tuna sandwich. I hated tuna. I hated the smell and the look of it. I hated that it could be kept in a can for years and never turn bad. Would that happen to me? Would I be kept here for years and never turn bad? I didn't think I was as lucky as a can of tuna and certainly wouldn't survive if I didn't eat so I begrudgingly picked up the sandwich and took a bite once he set it in front of me.

After I had choked down the last of it, Kaden took my plate and tossed it into the sink. He leaned back against the counter and stared at me from across the room.

"You want to tell me who your parents are?"

I shook my head.

"Do you want me to guess?"

I glared at him. *I was telling the truth,* I signed.

"Shit..." Kaden mumbled something about my handicap as he walked from the room. I sat there, unsure of what to do. I could call out his name but Ray would realize Kaden had been lying. As much as I disliked Kaden, I hated Ray even more. The man had been prepared to kill me in cold blood. Not a crime of passion, just a crime of convenience. I believed him capable of it.

Kaden returned with a piece of paper and a magic marker. "Write it down."

I picked up the pen and removed the cap. *I didn't lie.*

"Bullshit," Kaden spat at me.

I shrugged and sat back in my chair. In a flash, his hand was at the back of my head, gripping my hair and forcing my face down to the table. His lips came into view as he turned my head toward them.

"Write the fucking names, Raleigh!"

He pulled me back up and released my hair. My jaw clenched in anger but my hand gripped the pen in submission.

Clive and Meghan Winters

I pushed the paper away from me and threw the pen on the table. At least part of what I had written was true, and if he did any research at all he would learn that my mom and her husband had been killed in a car accident. My father's name would remain a secret until forced from me or discovered by other means.

Kaden took the paper and walked into the other room. A few moments later, I felt the floorboards shake as the front door closed. It didn't even cross my mind that Kaden would leave me alone in the house. Timidly, I stood up and walked around the corner, relieved to see Kaden standing in front of an open closet. I watched him pull some linens and a quilt from the top shelf. Then, as if he could feel me staring at him, he turned around.

"You can ask me why if you want."

I was curious but didn't expect an answer that I would like. "Why did you lie to them?"

"The more I know, the less I'll need them. Ray's foolish and acts before he thinks. His brother will follow him into anything."

So what was he planning on doing, ransoming me for the highest price and keeping everything for himself while the other two did the grunt work?

With his arms full of bedding, he started to walk toward me. "Does it upset you that I'm using you this way?" His smile dripped with contempt.

I shook my head. "Use me as much as you want. Just promise to let me go at the end and I'll play along with any game you want me to."

"Is that an invitation?"

"No," *You disgusting asshole.*

"Well, just so you're aware, Blondie, you need my protection just as much as I need your silence." He was standing within an arm's reach and if I hadn't been in such pain, I would have slapped him. I needed nothing, especially from him.

"You should learn to appreciate me and stop glaring like that." He shoved the sheets and quilt into my chest and I reflexively raised my arms to catch them before they fell.

Appreciate him? Appreciate had too nice a connotation. I felt as if I was in his debt because of what he had done. I certainly wasn't grateful for anything.

"I don't need your protection," I said as he stepped around me and opened a door. I peered inside and saw a staircase leading down to a dark room.

"After you," he waived me down and I hesitantly took the first few steps. It wasn't becoming any easier to see in the gloom of the basement, so I turned around to make sure Kaden was following me. His face was nothing but a shadow with the light of the upstairs on his back. His jaw was moving but I couldn't read his lips and with a frustrated groan, I continued down into the darkness.

There was only a sliver of light left when I reached the bottom of the stairs. I felt the cold pavement beneath my feet and smelled damp air, but beyond that, there was nothing. As soon as Kaden made it down, he nudged me out of the way and walked to a wall behind the stairs, disappearing into the darkness. Within seconds, a bulb above my head flickered and produced a dim glow, weak enough to leave a few corners of the basement in the shadows.

I looked around. There were no windows on the grey cinderblock walls, just old pieces of broken furniture leaning precariously against each other. A leak from the kitchen floor had stained the ceiling and dripped into a puddle on the floor. A black fridge was backed into one corner next to an old wash basin.

Kaden pulled an old, stained mattress from the wall, throwing it to the floor in the middle of the room. I dropped the bedding and knelt down beside the mattress, cautious to not hurt my ribs. The bed was dry but it had a strange smell. At least it was better than the floor. I started unfolding the sheets and fitting them to the mattress, wondering what Kaden was thinking. He wasn't helping me, but stood at one end of the bed with his arms crossed at his chest, just staring at me as I worked.

"What now?" I looked up at him once I was done. His green eyes narrowed and his muscles flexed.

"Nothing."

"Am I just supposed to stay down here?"

"Did you want to come upstairs? Maybe play a board game or watch a movie?" He smirked.

He terrified me as much as he intrigued me. I knew this man was dangerous and I wanted nothing more than to run away from him. But our scene in the bathroom kept replaying in my head. He so easily could have taken me, thrown me on the ground and forced himself on me completely. But he didn't. Either he didn't want to or he had stopped himself. Maybe he had been worried that Ray and his brother would hear. But if that was the case, why hadn't he tried anything since they left?

"Can I have my things back? I'd like to brush my teeth." I could still taste the tuna.

Kaden nodded toward the stairs and watched as I curled my feet beneath me, rolled onto my toes and stood up without bending my torso. He followed me up the stairs and trailed me into the bathroom. He stayed outside as I brushed my teeth and used the toilet, not letting me close the door all the way.

I stared into the mirror. The toothpaste scrubbed away the taste of the tuna and the grit of the previous day but it couldn't take away the feeling in the back of my throat. You know that slight choking feeling where you are afraid you will burst into tears at any moment? It had been there since I woke up in the trunk of the car and had yet to go away. My hair had dried into lose curls which hung around my face and neck. I hadn't worn my hair curly in years, relying daily on a straightening iron to smooth it out. My face was bruised along the hairline, above my right eye. My lips were still cracked and my cheeks were pale, but the look suited me at the moment. It exemplified everything I felt, everything I was thinking: scared and hurt, defeated and defenseless.

I turned away from the mirror and walked passed Kaden, back down the stairs to the entrance of the basement. I turned to him before I opened the door.

"Are you going to lock it behind me?"

"Yes," he answered plainly and without any sign of guilt.

"What if I need something?"

"You can wait until dinner."

I won't be hungry, I signed as I turned away from him and opened the door, slamming it behind me as I walked down the stairs. I kept the light on as I crawled into my bed, sleep finally pulling on me, begging me to let it take me away. I fell asleep watching the ceiling boards produce light clouds of dust as Kaden paced the floor above my head.

Chapter 5

I felt something brush against my leg and opened my eyes. I sat up, startled at the pitch black of the room, blinking furiously and trying to remember if I had turned off the lights. I hadn't. I felt heavy fingers searching for my leg in the darkness and I panicked. I kicked frantically and made contact with something warm and soft. Kaden hadn't felt like that when he had been holding me outside the car. I was about to scream for him to stop when I was startled by another set of hands groping my shoulders and wrapping around my neck. I started to scream but the hands tightened and my voice was lost in my chest.

A course and calloused hand traveled over my jaw and covered my mouth while the other tangled in my hair, pulling me back to the mattress. The hands at my feet gripped my ankles and moved up to my knees, impervious to my kicks and struggles. I felt long legs straddle my hips. His hands worked their way under my shirt and up to my chest. Finally, I screamed against the hand that was covering my mouth, still kicking and thrashing my arms around violently.

The old mattress only gave a little and the hands on my chest crushed me against it, making it difficult to breath. The hands fondled my breasts, pulling and pinching, and it wasn't long before I felt something warm and wet on my neck. A tongue slithered over my jaw and around my ear before replacing the hand over my mouth. I held my lips together as a tongue tried to enter my mouth, my fists still beating furiously against a chest and shoulders, taking random swings at the second man who held me down. The attacker didn't seem to notice in the slightest as he turned and twisted my breasts beneath his massive hands.

I stopped my efforts and hesitated when I felt his tongue leave my face. I didn't want to scream because I could still feel his breath on my lips. The warm air coming from his mouth was accompanied by a light spray of saliva and I could only guess what he was screaming. Suddenly, a sharp pain stabbed my ribcage as a fist made contact with my side. I gasped in pain. That was the window he was looking for and I felt a thick tongue slide into my mouth, sour breath nearly causing me to gag. I turned my head to escape his lips, but to no avail. One of his hands left my breast and traveled to my jeans, fumbling with the button and zipper before plunging beneath the denim and prodding at my panties. I didn't know what to do. I couldn't fight him off, couldn't save myself. So I did the next thing that came to mind. I bit down hard, waiting until I tasted blood before releasing, and screaming at the top of my lungs in the hopes that someone would hear me.

A hand struck my face and I felt blood splatter on my skin as he spit on me. As he smacked my face with the back of his hand again, I saw a hazy light fill the room. My eyes adjusted slowly, my head dizzy from the blows. It was Ray. His face was still close to mine but he wasn't looking at me. I nearly gagged again when I saw how much blood there was beneath the stubble on his chin. I turned my head to follow his gaze and saw a blurry Kaden standing in front of us, his face red and his hand clenched.

"Get off of her," Kaden said, looking straight at Ray.

I didn't look up to see Ray's response.

"Fuck you! Get off!" Kaden's eyes continued to bore into Ray.

Neither man spoke and the room filled with a heated tension. Ray's brother released his grip on my hair and the mattress heaved as he stood up. I craned my neck so I could see him. His brown eyes stared looked regretful. He didn't look a day over eighteen in this light and I almost pitied him and his role in all of this.

Ray was still on top of me. He stared back at Kaden with a playful bullishness, although I couldn't tell if he was challenging or propositioning my defender. Slowly, his head started to shake, his round face moving closer to mine.

"Did you want to go first?" he asked. "Who fucks her first probably doesn't matter to her."

I looked at Kaden. "Get off," he repeated.

"But she's perfect," Ray protested and looked down at me as his hand came out from under my shirt and stroked my hair. "You can do whatever you want to her and won't have to listen to her bitching when it's over."

My jaw clenched. I was dying to scream at him, to tell him what a sick, twisted, disgusting excuse for a man he was. But I didn't. My eyes burned into his with all of the hatred I had for him and all of the contempt I felt toward Kaden for getting me to play along with this lie. Ray smiled and his thin and bloodstained lips crept over his yellow teeth. His fingers twitched beneath my jeans and I twisted by body in a lame attempt to escape.

"She's wet, too. Wet and ready for us. What a fucking whore."

It wasn't true, though. I knew it and by the look on Kaden's face he knew it too. But why wasn't he doing anything? Why was he just standing there, allowing Ray to continue?

I felt Ray's fingers start to move back and forth across my panties and the humiliation became more than I could stand. A wave of nausea swept over me and tears slid down my cheeks. I was almost ready to give up and accept my fate, convinced that Kaden wasn't going to do anything more to stop Ray's assault.

"So what do you say, Kaden?" Ray spoke again. "Shall we go at her from both ends? Plug her until she pops?"

Kaden lunged at Ray. His green eyes blazed with anger and his mouth twisted into a snarl. Ray landed hard on my stomach but quickly rolled to the side as Kaden's body came down on him. I backed up quickly, freeing my legs from beneath the squabble of limbs. Two hands pulled me up. Kaden delivered his first punch to Ray's face. Ray fought desperately to block him but Kaden was quick and landed another blow to the side of Ray's jaw.

Suddenly, Kaden stood up and backed away. Ray lay on his back and was holding his side, laughing. Kaden panted, out of breath.

"You better watch yourself, Kaden. We're in this together, all equal shares, remember? That includes her."

"Go find some girl in town to fuck, Ray. You can't have her." Kaden pointed to me as he spoke and then turned his full attention to the man holding me. "The same goes for you, Marshal, although I doubt you have it in you."

Marshal dropped his hands from my arms and walked toward the stairs.

"Who are you to tell me what I can and cannot have?" Ray asked as he stood up and brushed himself off. He zipped his fly and buttoned the top of his jeans.

"I'm the one who just kicked your ass." He rolled his shoulders forward and stood up straight. "Don't touch her again."

"Come on, man. It's not worth it," Marshal pleaded with his brother.

Ray shot Kaden one last warning glare before he nodded and pushed past him to follow his brother up the stairs. Kaden watched them leave before looking at me. His face showed little emotion and his eyes were like glass.

"Are you all right?"

Fuck you, I signed, completely outraged he would bother asking such a question.

"Did he hurt you?" Kaden didn't seem to take offense.

Yes. My sides ached and my face felt swollen but what was he going to do about it?

He nodded and walked slowly toward me, pulling at the bottom of his shirt. I stepped back as he neared, not wanting anything or anyone to come within an arm's length of me. But Kaden held up his hand in surrender, the other bringing the tail of his shirt up to his ribs. I eyed him cautiously and he paused before stripping off his shirt. I took a few more steps back, shaking my head, signing for him not to come any closer.

"I'm not going to hurt you, Raleigh. I won't even touch you."

I was backed up against the wall with no place to go. Kaden slowly closed the space between us. My breath came out short and weak, I didn't have any fight left in me, so, with tears in my eyes, I gave up. He lifted his balled shirt and brought it to my cheek. I was scared he was going to gag me with it, blindfold me perhaps, but he didn't. Carefully and softly, he wiped away Ray's blood from my face and neck.

I looked down once I realized what he had started doing and felt the tiniest twinge of guilt for not trusting him. But why should I? He wasn't my friend or necessarily even on my side. I was being used by this man. But maybe even if I couldn't trust him, I might be able to trust his motives. Did that even make any sense?

Staring at Kaden's naked chest did little to help my confusion. His large muscles flexed as he worked to clean my face. His smooth skin was pulled over defined abdominals and a faint trail of hair progressed from his lower stomach only to disappear beneath his belt. His other hand leaned against the wall to support his weight, trapping me between his body and the cinderblocks.

I longed to be comforted. I wanted him to touch me, to tell me everything was going to be alright, to take me in his arms and keep me there until all the pain went away. I could feel his body warmth and it tempted me to reach out and run my hands over his skin, pull him close and hold on tight. But I didn't move. Kaden would never comfort me. I was nothing but a dollar sign to him.

He finally finished cleaning my face and I raised my head to look at him. He studied his work carefully, his eyes roaming my face but never meeting my gaze, his lips staying firmly pressed together, and his eyebrows furrowed in concentration. He pulled his hand away from the wall and he seemed to reach for me, nearing but not quite touching my skin. I wanted to lean into it, force him to touch me but I kept still. Our eyes met for a second before he pulled his hand away.

I took a deep breath. He turned away and I repressed the urge to thank him. Not looking back, he skipped up the stairs two at a time, the spring in his step emphasizing how ready he was to be away from me. I pushed myself from the wall, my knees shaking and my heart thudding in my chest. I climbed back into bed, pulled the covers up to my neck, and cried myself back to sleep.

Chapter 6

"Can you hear her?"

I giggled and looked up at my father. "Yes. She sounds beautiful."

He smiled down at me and took my little hand in his, leading me quickly down the hallway of the opera house. The grand door opened quietly and we slipped inside unnoticed. I ran as fast as my short, pudgy legs could carry me to the front row, my mother smiling at me from the stage as she sang. Her voice filled the enormous space and I took a seat directly in front of her so I could watch every move. She slid gracefully across the stage, her arms stretched wide and her generous hips swaying in time with the music. I couldn't understand what she was singing; my father had told me I wouldn't because it was in French. But I didn't mind. My mother's voice was the most beautiful thing in the world and I let it fill my ears and heart completely.

The song finished and I stood up and cheered, my mother beaming at me. "Tell me, Darling, what did you think?"

"I loved it!" I exclaimed as I jumped up and down, eager to show my approval.

"Shall we sing one together, then?"

"Mama, I don't know any from this one," I explained, hoping she wouldn't mind and ask me again despite this drawback.

"But you know so many others. Come on stage and we'll sing together." She smiled at me and I ran up the stairs and across the stage into her waiting arms. She brushed a blonde curl out of my face before hugging me close and kissing my cheek.

"Now, what shall it be? 'You Are My Sunshine?' 'Lullaby and Goodnight?'"

"'Baby Mine!'"

"'Baby Mine' it is then." My mother stood up and I did the same, throwing my shoulders back and opening my rib cage, just like she showed me.

"Daddy, are you watching?" My eyes scanned the empty chairs and found him sitting a few rows back, a wide smile on his face as he stared up at his two girls.

"I'm watching, Baby." I couldn't tell if he was speaking to me or my mother but I smiled and looked up to see her winking at him.

My mother didn't mind my shrill singing. She always told me how wonderful I sounded and today was no different. I was the picture of happiness as she reached down to hug me.

"You go join your father now, I have to finish the rehearsal."

I nodded and skipped off the stage, turning halfway up the isle to wave at her and blow a kiss. I reached my father in the back of the auditorium, his protective hand resting on my shoulder.

I woke up. Kaden stood over me kicking the mattress. He was frowning and had a bowl in his hand. I could see steam rising from the top.

"Oatmeal."

Of course it was oatmeal. Couldn't he say something normal such as 'Good morning' or 'I've brought you breakfast?' I sat up, the pain in my chest much better than the day before, and threw my legs over the side of the mattress. Kaden handed me the bowl and walked up the stairs without saying another word. I waited until he was out of sight before devouring the warm breakfast. It was instant oatmeal, that much was clear, but I didn't care. It was enough to get me through the morning.

When I finished, I stood up and looked around. Last night's terror still fogged my head, making it difficult for me to breathe, difficult to think, difficult to stay standing and not throw myself back to the bed. New tears fell from my eyes but I was determined to stay strong. Kaden had stopped them and I was safe for now. I took two hesitant steps forward, feeling as if I was walking for the first time, and then took I took a few more.

I circled the room, examining everything that was now in my world. The faucet on the wash basin was rusted. I turned the knobs and a thick, brown stream of water flowed into the drain. I let it run for a few moments and it eventually turned clear although I didn't trust it enough to drink it. Next, I opened the fridge and was hit with a foul smell. Molded fruit and leftovers lay inside along with a few beers on the door.

Turning around, I walked to the stairs and peered up, surprised to find the door had been left open. I grabbed my toothbrush and climbed slowly up the rickety wooden staircase, waiting for one of the trembling boards to crack under my feet. I stepped hesitantly into the bright living room, unsure of who I would find. I had lost all sense of time in the windowless basement and the clock on the wall read 10:45.

Kaden sat at the table, a laptop open in front of him, and an angry expression on his face. He didn't look at me as I entered the room although I know he heard me. His green eyes glowed in the reflection of the screen, and his full lips were pursed tightly together.

I knew he was probably investigating my family, searching to find which relative could pay the most for my safe return. But I didn't want to be there if he happened to stumble upon my father's name. I took my toothbrush and walked up stairs to the bathroom. The window had been boarded shut. Even though the house now felt more like a prison, at least I was able to roam it freely.

I felt sick when I looked at my face in the mirror. My already bruised and beaten face was now swollen around my eyes. I stripped my clothes off and turned on the water in the shower. I lathered my body with soap, washed my hair repeatedly, and then lathered my body again. But nothing could wash away the feeling of Ray's hands on my skin or his tongue on my face.

When I was done, I opened the shower curtain and screamed, jumping back against the wall as I saw Kaden's infuriated face inches from mine.

What are you doing? I signed to him when I had control of my shaking hands.

"Tell me, Raleigh, what about this don't you understand? Keeping these secrets from me isn't going to help you."

I don't know...

"Speak! They're fucking gone!"

"I don't know what you're talking about," I lied as I reached for my towel from the day before. Kaden grabbed it and threw it at me, throwing up his hands in frustration.

"This isn't funny. If Ray and Marshal find out who your father is, we're fucked."

"No, I'm already fucked," I snapped at him. "You've kidnapped me, remember? Regardless of if they find out or not, this isn't going to go well for me."

"It will go a lot better if you do exactly what I say and stop lying."

"Why should I do anything you say?" I challenged him although I already knew the answer.

He grabbed my arm and brought his face closer to mine. "You want a repeat of last night? Maybe next time, I won't hear you scream."

My face became solemn and I looked away. "I don't want that to happen again," I finally admitted.

Kaden's fingers turned my head toward his. "I won't let it. Just tell me if there is anything else you're keeping from me."

I shook my head. He didn't want my whole life story. He wanted money and now he knew exactly where he could get it. I don't know if he realized the boat he was throwing himself into. A senator's daughter, even one that hasn't been able to maintain a functional relationship with her father since age six, wasn't someone to be toyed with. The resources at my father's disposal were almost endless and Kaden was going to be lucky if he was able to outsmart them.

"Get dressed and come downstairs. We've got a lot to talk about." He released my arm and left me standing in the shower. A clean shirt had replaced the blood stained one he had given me yesterday and was neatly folded on the ground next to my jeans.

I dressed quickly and walked downstairs. Kaden sat the computer. I sat down across from him and watched him read the article on the screen. I prayed it wasn't one of the archived tabloid reports of my adolescent behavior. Eventually, he closed the browser and stared at me.

"You're father is said to be a favorite of the GOP."

I nodded.

"Senator Christopher Chapman comes from a long line of political figures but is the first to be a Senator."

I blinked.

"What would he do if he knew his daughter was kidnapped while hitchhiking in North Carolina?"

I looked away, afraid to answer. My father would do anything he could to get me back. That was his obligation. If the press found out, he might act, in front of the cameras at least, like he wanted me back. But I was a burden to him, a rebel child who challenged his conservative ideals. He had, over the course of my twenty-six years, paid me to keep quiet and out of the spotlight. To everybody who mattered, I was the ideal daughter. One even to be pitied because of my handicap.

I looked back at Kaden who waited for my response.

"He would want me back."

"Does he know where you are?"

I shook my head. My father thought I was in Europe visiting museums. I had cashed in my graduation present (first class tickets to Rome) and packed my bag, hitching a ride from the airport. With nowhere in particular to go and months of freedom ahead of me, I had traveled from Delaware all the way to North Carolina courtesy of truckers and lonely drivers. Sure, it was dangerous, but after graduating with a degree that I had no desire to use, I was longing for a little excitement.

"Does he know who you were with?" Kaden asked.

"Julie? Does he know I was with Julie, the woman you killed with your car?"

Kaden answered with a glare.

"No," I admitted. "I met her in Tennessee."

"You don't like your father, do you?" He asked without pause.

Now it was my turn to glare. "What does it matter?"

"Let me guess, your father fell in love with your mother, the beautiful and vibrant opera singer from London, but couldn't handle the stress of juggling a family and his career so he left you and your mother with a large monthly allowance to keep you happy?"

"Something like that."

"Something but not quiet?" Kaden raised an eyebrow in curiosity.

"I remember us being happy. Until I lost my hearing, we were happy. He could handle anything and everything until that was taken away from me."

"What happened?" Kaden looked genuinely interested, an expression which I hadn't seen before.

"Measles."

"I thought there were vaccinations for that."

"My mother didn't believe in them. He blamed her for the disease."

"And now you're angry because she's dead and he uses your disadvantage to advance his political career."

"Yes. And now you're scared because ransoming a senator's daughter is going to be a lot harder than ransoming off a lonely hitchhiker."

Kaden raised an eyebrow and we stared at each other for a minute. He had such intuition about me it was almost scary. I was amazed at how much he could learn from a few hours on the Internet and a few minutes in my company.

"You don't even want to go home, do you, Raleigh?"

That bastard. *I just want to leave here,* I signed, not wanting him to hear me say it.

Good luck trying.

I turned away, unable to look at him any longer. I didn't know what life was going to be like here. I didn't know if I could expect Ray and his pathetic younger brother to attack me every night. I didn't know if Kaden would tire of protecting me and say to hell with it. Maybe he would let Ray kill me if things didn't go his way.

Kaden's hips and torso came into view as I stared off into nothing, thinking about my future. I turned my neck more so I didn't have to look at him but, like he always did when he had something to say, his fingers gripped my face and turned my head up toward his. He looked incredibly tall from where I sat, his dark hair falling in his eyes and his shoulders curling over his chest.

"It could be a lot worse," he said slowly and moved a step closer, putting a hand on my shoulder to keep me in place. His belt buckle was at eye level and one more step would have eliminated the distance completely.

"I could be making you do things they don't even talk about in your Ivy League schools."

My jaw clenched and I smiled at him. "It was George Washington University, actually."

Kaden scoffed and released my face, walking away and sitting on the couch. He picked up a remote and turned on the small television that was in the corner of the room. I stood up, not wanting to join him, just wanting to do something to distract myself, but he spread his legs on the couch, leaving no room for me even if I had wanted to sit down. Shaking my head and rolling my eyes, I walked to the kitchen and looked under the sink. There, along with old grocery bags and a pair of snow boots, was exactly what I was looking for. I picked up the bleach, the tile cleaner and a sponge before standing up and turning straight into Kaden.

"What do you think you're doing?"

"Cleaning. This place is as disgusting as you are."

Kaden's emerald eyes sparkled with amusement and his lips twitched into a half smile. "Don't make yourself too useful. I might never let you go."

"Good luck explaining that to the FBI agents who will be pounding down your door when they discover I'm missing. Time's running out rather quickly now. I haven't spoken to my father in almost a week and he'll begin to wonder where I am."

"Fuck you, Raleigh," Kaden swore before walking back into the living room and taking his position on the couch.

I smiled to myself and for the first time in many, many years, I was happy that my father was in such a position of power.

Chapter 7

The hours felt like days and the days felt like months. I spent most of my time in the basement, cleaning and organizing, trying to keep myself busy because the alternative was lonely misery. At times I would find tears on my cheeks without even realizing I had been crying. I would drop a glass or a towel, whatever else was in my hand, without even realizing I was shaking.

Kaden stayed true to his word and kept Ray away from me. On the days when Ray and his brother left the house, Kaden would keep the basement door open. I was free to roam around the main floor, and use the kitchen and bathroom as I pleased. I looked forward to those days.

But on days when they were all away, or on days when they all stayed in the house, the basement door would remain locked and I had nothing but myself and the broken furniture to keep me entertained. Often, I would try to imagine the furniture in its prime, what it looked like, where it was kept, what was stored in the drawers or beneath table legs. Unfortunately, my imagination was not very creative and all the images inside my head looked more like a shabby-chic collection from a design catalogue. Other times, I would lie in my bed and try to remember my mother's voice. Although I doubted I was remembering it accurately; it had been such a long time since I had heard anything.

I was doing just that, while staring at the basement ceiling, when I saw the dust falling from the beams overhead and I knew they were home. A week, maybe eight or nine days, had passed since they first brought me here, and I knew Kaden was getting anxious. He would stare at me for literally hours on end if we were alone, trying to figure out what he was going to do with me. His gaze bothered me at first but, like the silence, I learned to get used to it. I was never doing anything amusing or entertaining - usually just reading whatever magazine Ray or Marshal brought home. They had no books. Sometimes I would watch television with him - Kaden's green eyes were always on me, studying and questioning my every move.

We rarely spoke, which I found odd. If I were in his position, I would want to know everything I could about the person I was planning to ransom. I took his silence to be some sort of strategy, some plan to keep me scared and submissive. On the rare occasions when we did speak to one another, his questions and statements tended to be little more than one or two word phrases such as 'hungry?' or 'nice day.' It wasn't much, but at least it was human interaction.

Suddenly, the light in the room became brighter and I looked toward the stairs, knowing the door had been opened. Kaden's now familiar red Pumas came into sight as he staggered down the stairs. Was he drunk? His steps were usually so confident. As he came closer, I saw that I had been correct; he had a beer in one hand and was struggling to hold onto the railing with the other. His green eyes, normally bright and knowing, were glazed over and his lids were heavy.

He came to a stop on the bottom stair and just looked at me, blinking slowly and swaying on his feet.

"Do you know what you've done to me?" He wasn't opening his lips very wide and it was hard for me to determine what he was saying.

No, I signed, hoping he would do the same.

"You've taken over my life. You're all I think about and I can't get you out of my fucking head!"

I didn't respond.

"You should be gone by now. I should have let Ray kill you but I was stupid and selfish, thinking I could ..."

He took a step toward me but tripped down the last stair, landing on his knees and breaking the bottle of beer in his hand. He didn't attempt to stand up, but crawled over to my bed. I backed to the far side of the mattress, ready to jump up and run if necessary.

Kaden laughed. "Don't bother trying to escape. The guys upstairs won't be any help."

I glared at him and he smiled.

"Do you still hate me after all this time? I wish I could hate you, Raleigh, but I can't." He pulled himself onto the mattress and stretched his legs so he was lying on his side facing me.

"I try to hate you because, really, all you are is just some stuck up bitch with too much of Daddy's money. You wouldn't even give a guy like me a passing glance if we met on the street."

That much was probably true. But I couldn't think about what would have happened if Kaden and I met under different circumstances. That didn't help me in my present situation.

Kaden moved closer to me and reached for my arm. I jerked away. But he was too quick and had me by the wrist, pulling me back to the mattress before I could stand up. His strong arms hauled me under him as he rolled on top of me, pinning me to the sheets, his hands at my shoulders and his knees on the outside of my thighs.

I remained absolutely frozen. His eyes danced over my face, the muscles in his arms flexing as he gripped my shoulders tightly.

"So, maybe," he continued. "Maybe all I have to do is have you once and I'll be able to forget you."

His face started to come down toward mine and he kept staring into my eyes, waiting to see if I would protest.

"I can't promise you're going to like it, but I'll try not to hurt you."

Then, before I could turn my face to avoid his mouth, he kissed me. His full lips molded around mine and forced them apart. I could taste the beer on his breath, but his tongue was sweet as it gently entered my mouth. Kaden's fingers softly touched my cheek and neck, running down my arms and across my sides. I waited for his hands to roam but they stayed fixed, one gripping the fabric of my t-shirt, and the other gently touching my face.

This kiss hadn't been what I expected. I closed my eyes and realized how easy it was to imagine it all happening under different circumstances. Kaden kissed me again and again, each time as gentle and eager as the time before. He would tenderly bite my lower lip, tease my tongue with his, and then close his lips only to start again.

The realization that I was kissing him back hit us both simultaneously. My eyes flew open and he pulled away quickly, leaving me feeling naked without his warm body. Sitting above my knees, he stared at me, his eyes no longer glossy, and his lustful expression mixed with confusion. I pushed myself up onto my elbows, breathing heavily, but not wanting him to see me in a completely submissive position. I couldn't apologize because I didn't want to appear weak. I couldn't admit what I had done, because I didn't want him to think he had that much persuasion over me. So I stared at him, challenging him to make the next move.

Kaden opened his mouth to speak and then shut it, pushing away from the mattress and running up the stairs. The door slammed, shaking the banister and I threw myself back on the mattress, staring at the clouds of dust raining down from the ceiling.

Chapter 8

I slept very little that night, replaying the kiss in my mind, each time creating a new outcome and willing it to be true. But I knew what had happened. Kaden had kissed me and I had kissed him back. I was such a fool, so caught up in the moment, and now he had something to use against me.

I wasn't at all surprised to see Marshal tiptoeing down the stairs to deliver my breakfast the next morning. Did he think I would hear him? The kid handed me the oatmeal, looking confused and shy.

Thank you, I signed, smiling more at his awkward demeanor than his act of bringing me breakfast.

"You're welcome," he replied, though he looked as if he were asking a question with his eyebrow raised and his head tilted slightly to one side.

You're welcome, I signed back.

Marshal grinned back at me as he repeated the motion. I nodded in approval and his smile widened. He quickly turned to leave, shutting the door on his way out.

And so the days passed. On my way to the bathroom and again on my way back to the basement, I would see Kaden and Ray sitting in the living room, rarely doing anything that looked productive or strategic. Kaden never looked at me, and although it pained me to admit it, I was upset by it. So I spent the days in the basement, lying on my mattress, imagining possible escape scenarios, all of which I deemed implausible or too dangerous.

My meals became fewer and farther between; often all I received was my morning oatmeal, usually delivered by Marshal. I learned to ration it throughout my day. On my infrequent trips to the bathroom, I could see myself wasting away, my skin turning grey and my spirit draining. Showers were the worst because I noticed my hipbones sharply jutting from my waist. My hair fell out in small clumps when I ran my fingers through it, and the veins on my arms and hands protruded from my skin.

I'm not sure how much time had passed since Kaden had spoken to me. I lived in silence and the lack of conversation was torture. I didn't dare speak out loud to either Marshal or Ray, choosing to believe that Kaden wouldn't break his promise. I found myself, unable to talk with anyone else, having conversations with my reflection. I would sign, of course, not trusting my voice enough to whisper. Some days I would encourage myself to stay strong, others I would retell my favorite childhood memories or favorite fairy tales. It was during one of those stories that Kaden decided to speak to me again.

I saw the door open in the mirror, my hands instantly becoming rigid at my side. I turned to face whoever was interrupting me. Kaden stood on the other side of the doorframe, his face a mixture of confusion and frustration, his body tall and stiff.

"I came to check on you. You've been up here a while."

Afraid I slit my wrist or hung myself with shoestrings?

"You can speak, they've left for the day."

But I didn't want to say anything to him. I turned around and picked up my brush, running in through my hair and wincing as it pulled out strand after strand of blonde curls. Kaden stared at my reflection in the mirror, his face appeared concerned. He turned slowly and left, leaving me to finish my daily routine alone.

I couldn't decide if I wanted to stay or leave once I reached the living room on my way back to the basement. The light coming through the windows was pleasant, but Kaden's muscular body on the couch was a grueling reminder of my captivity. I chose to stay when I glanced at the paper on the table. It had been so long since I had seen a newspaper; I jumped at the chance to read it.

I sat down and picked it up; the first thing I looked for was the date. October 10th. I had been here five weeks. I closed my eyes and tried to imagine a different time, tried to imagine what I would be doing at this very moment had we never been hit by Ray and his car. But my imagination let me down for I could not even envision myself outside of this house. I shook my head and moved past the thought. Counting the hours and the days would only make my imprisonment seem longer. My eyes scanned the page and the picture at the bottom caught my attention. A woman with light hair and large eyes stared up at me. She wore baggy jeans and a Rolling Stones t-shirt. It was Julie.

But before I could read the article, Kaden snatched the paper from my hand and crumpled it into a ball. He glared at me.

"Give that back."

"Nice try." Kaden laughed in my face but I knew better. Behind the smile, his eyes were scared.

"Time really is running out, isn't it?"

"You don't know what you saw," he replied and walked away from me, no longer laughing.

"They found her, didn't they?" But he wouldn't turn around. "Let's see, they must have found her body and assumed she had drowned, but upon further investigation, realized she had been thrown in the water post mortem. I guess it's only a matter of time before someone sees that paper and is able to identify the last person with whom she was seen alive. That would be me, in case you hadn't figured it out."

He balled his fists and his muscles flexed.

"Shut the fuck up, Raleigh! You don't know anything!"

"Fine. But I'm guessing my twenty five thousand dollars is looking pretty nice right about now. Or were you hoping my father could speak to the President and work out something a little more substantial?"

He took three or four large steps toward me, pointing his finger in my face and clenching his jaw. "You haven't said a word in over three weeks and now you think you can come downstairs and frighten me with your pathetic assumptions? You need to remember that you have no say in any of this and I can kill you or let Ray have his way with you, whenever I please."

"So do it," I spat back at him. "Kill me. Or better yet, let Ray do it. Show him how wrong you really were in taking me that night. Show him that you can't go through with whatever lame plan you two have hatched. It really doesn't matter to me because I will be happy knowing that no matter if I live or if I die, you will get caught."

"Shut your fucking mouth!"

"Or what? You'll threaten me some more?" I scoffed and looked away. If I had known just how badly I had set him off, I would never have dreamed of pushing him that far. But it was too late. Kaden's fingers were around my jaw, jerking my face toward his.

"I will teach you to keep that mouth shut, Raleigh. I won't let you forget who has the upper hand in this relationship."

He grabbed my arm and heaved his shoulder into my side, hoisting me up and throwing me over his back. I wiggled and flailed my arms and legs but his grasp was too strong. He carried me up the stairs, easily subduing me.

My screams and demands to be released were pointless. I used my fists to beat Kaden's back but it was no use. We reached the landing of the stairs and, instead of carrying me down the hallway to the bathroom, he turned and went in the direction of a closed door. I had often wondered where the three men slept, noting the different hallways and doors that could lead to possible bedrooms or closets. But, even if I had let my curiosity get the better of me, one of them was usually watching and would never have allowed me to open the wrong door.

Kaden carried me into a room, and my hands gripping the doorframe. I held on with all my strength but he was too powerful and I screamed in terror at the force he used to pull me inside. My arms reached in vain for something else to grab, but they found nothing. He threw me into the air and I landed on a soft mattress, my head hitting the wall behind the bed.

Kaden tugged his shirt over his head, his chest and stomach heaving from anger and exertion. I pushed away as far as I could, my back pressed against the wall, but his hands were quick and around my ankle before I could kick them away. With one strong tug, my body went flying toward his. He descended on me like an eagle would its prey, his hands spread wide while his body quickly but gracefully bent down toward mine.

I struggled to turn onto my stomach, attempting to crawl away from the beast of a man, but the smooth satin finish of the comforter provided little traction and all I managed to do was pull the top layer back from the pillows. Kaden's hard torso pressed against my back and he yanked my hips from the bed. One strong arm came under my stomach to hold me up and the free hand nimbly freed the button of my jeans and released the zipper.

I clawed at the mattress, having already pulled all of the sheets and fittings away.

"Please, don't do this," I begged, still too terrified to cry. But Kaden's large hands quickly had my jeans below my hips and around my knees. He ripped my underwear off in one strong swoop of his hand and I screamed again for him to stop. "No!"

I pushed my body flat against the bed in a last attempt at self preservation, but once again, Kaden's hands pulled at my waist, bringing my hips off the mattress and into his naked stomach. He felt warm against my bare skin but didn't stay that way for long. His fingers tangled in my hair, gripping hard enough to pull my head back, his elbow in the crook of my vaulted back. I waited, my craned neck and arched spine making it hard to breathe and impossible to move, but soon I felt the mattress shake as he climbed onto the bed behind me. His knees spread my thighs as wide as my jeans would allow and then I felt his fingers, wet with his own saliva no doubt, stroking between my legs.

"Please stop," I whimpered between my feeble cries, closing my eyes and fighting to forget the pain in my back and neck.

His fingers rolled between my clenched lips and pushed deep inside of me only once before being replaced by something much larger. I could feel his impatience and I screamed, rolling my hips under to postpone the inevitable. With one hand, he lifted me from the bed completely, as he forced himself into me with one powerful movement. The pain and the humiliation silenced my cries as the air caught in my throat.

I tried not to feel anything as Kaden pulled my hips against his, deeper this time and with more conviction. But that was impossible. He filled me completely. "Please don't do this," I begged again, although I knew it was past the point of mattering.

He pulled my hair back and pounded into me for a third time.

"Kaden, please?" I croaked from my strained throat.

Without warning he pulled out entirely and released my hair, flipping me onto my back and pinning me down by my shoulders.

"What did you say?"

I blinked, unable to react to his question. His face was so close and so incredibly difficult to read that I couldn't tell if I had offended him or appeased to him.

"What did you say?" he repeated, his eyes closing as he screamed.

"I said, 'please,'" I repeated, my mouth still dry.

But Kaden shook his head. "No, you said my name."

I turned my head away, trying to remember if that was true. I had said it to myself so many times before but had never spoken it aloud.

"Say it again," he commanded as his fingers turned my face back toward his. His green eyes bore into mine so deeply that I couldn't refuse.

"Kaden," I said, using as little of my voice as possible. But that was all he needed. His lips were on mine before I could take a breath and his hands worked to free my knees from my pants.

His kiss wasn't how I remembered it; this one was forceful and demanding. But he tasted the same. His tongue danced with mine while he pushed my t-shirt up my chest. He pulled away, sitting up and tugging the shirt over my head, throwing it on the ground next to the bed.

My pants were next as he guided each knee up and out of the denim.

"Again," he repeated.

"Kaden." I took a deep breath. He was kneeling in between my legs, which he had spread wide with his knees, and staring down at me with a crooked smile on his perfect face. I stared back at him, waiting for him to do something. His piercing eyes never wavered as he hooked his arms under my knees and brought my hips off the bed.

I wanted to look away, but I was terrified I would miss something, some chance at escape, some glimpse of sympathy from him. Kaden started again slowly and deliberately. I felt everything. My arms were useless and sprawled to my sides, my hands lightly gripping the comforter as he held my gaze. His face was full of emotion and concentration. Clearly enjoying himself, his mouth stayed curled in a slight smile and his eyes sparkled with anticipation.

I wish I could have felt the same. But I only wanted it to be over. I didn't want to like it, I wanted to hate it, but as he started to move, my senses became sharper, my body reacting against the better judgment of my mind. Kaden must have known that I was fighting this, but he also knew that part of me couldn't deny him even if I wanted to.

All too soon, my eyelids became heavy and my unwanted pleasure began to peak. I so badly wanted to squeeze them shut and scream out his name, but I fought it with every ounce of energy that I had, and continued staring into Kaden's green eyes. My legs started to tingle as heat spread from my womb, my toes curled, and my fingers clenched the bedding beneath me.

"Don't fight it," Kaden smirked. He showed no signs of stopping, not even a sign of fatigue.

"I...I can't..." But I couldn't finish my sentence. I didn't even know what I had wanted to say.

I felt one of his hands move from my hip to my inner thigh. "I told you I would make you scream," Kaden said pressing his thumb between my legs. He didn't move his finger, just let the motion of his body pounding into mine create the friction he desired.

It was more than I could endure. The heat spread throughout my body, my eyes closed involuntarily, and I finally cried out in pleasure. My reaction was so intense that through my convulsions, I didn't even feel Kaden pull out only to finish on my stomach. The hot, sticky substance was a tangible reminder of the fight he had won. He had taken whatever confidence and innocence, I still possessed.

I opened my eyes watched him bend over and pull up his boxers, the sight of his naked body terrifying but impressive. He caught me staring and bent over to pick up his shirt from the floor.

"Clean yourself off," he commanded, throwing his shirt at me.

I sat up and looked away from him, picking up the shirt and wiping off my stomach. My hands were still shaking slightly, a shameful side effect of the climax. Kaden handed me my clothes, a hint of concern in his eyes, as he finally looked at my nearly naked body on his bed.

I dressed quickly, conscious of his eyes on me the entire time. He was still standing in his boxers when I finished, his body gleaming with a thin layer of sweat, his hair pushed from his face. He opened the door to his bedroom and nodded for me to leave. I practically ran from the room, down the stairs and into the basement. I knew Kaden was behind me. I knew he would be locking the door as I descended the stairs into the dim light of my room.

I threw myself onto my bed, crying in heavy, painful sobs that shook the mattress. Kaden had known me completely, touched nearly every inch of my body, but I had never felt so alone. I felt that if I didn't have someone to comfort me, someone to hold me and cradle away my fears, I would melt away into the cement floor of the basement, never to be seen again. I wasn't thinking about what had just happened, how I had been taken without my consent, how the pleasure I experienced was more humiliating than the act itself. No, I was only feeling abandoned.

Chapter 9

Tears still fell from my eyes as I stared at the ceiling that night. No one had bothered to bring me dinner and my stomach ached. I could tell they were all upstairs - the dust falling from above was heavier than normal and I wondered what they could be doing. Had Kaden told them about Julie? Perhaps he was trying to convince them to take the twenty five thousand dollars.

The sense of abandonment I had felt earlier in the day only increased with time. Kaden had promised to keep me safe from Ray but I had no one to keep me safe from Kaden. Being raped wasn't something I liked to think about, but being raped by Ray was almost an unbearable thought. What made Kaden a more agreeable rapist was what confused me.

I was so absorbed in my thoughts that I didn't notice Kaden walking down the stairs. His shadow passed over my eyes and I looked up, startled.

"Ray wants to ask you a few questions," he said, standing above me, his arms crossed at his chest.

I stared at him. *What kind of questions?* I signed.

"About the other girl. About who saw you together."

Does he know about my father?

"No, he thinks both of your parents are dead."

I stood up and shrugged my shoulders. If Kaden wanted to keep things from Ray, he must have some sort of plan. Since this plan no longer benefited me, I was going to do anything I could to sabotage it.

"Let's go upstairs, then," I said.

Kaden's hand was over my mouth in a flash, his eyes full of surprise and anger. "You keep your mouth shut, you understand me?"

I answered him with a glare. Of course I understood him, but I no longer cared.

"Look," he took a deep breath and released my face. "I can't change what happened this morning. You got everything you deserved, but Ray won't stop where I did. He'll kill you."

Maybe he will and maybe he won't. Daddy's money may appeal to him, too.

"It will, trust me. But then he'll realize the trouble that comes with it and get scared."

Why don't you just take the twenty five thousand and be done with me? You and I both know you won't get any more without an added bonus of a prison cell.

Kaden's eyes squinted with what looked like pain and perhaps a little anxiety. "I'm not ready to give up yet. I want more time."

I shrugged my shoulders. Time was not taking sides in this case. The longer I stayed here, the more degradation I was subjected to, and the less his chance of not getting caught. Kaden reached for my arm but I pushed past him, stomping up the stairs and into the living room.

Ray sat at the table with the crumpled newspaper in front of him. He looked up when he heard me coming and stood, towering over me even from across the room. His dark eyes glared at me and his round face was red with frustration.

"How well did you know this girl?"

What girl? I signed. Kaden translated.

"This girl!" Ray picked up the paper and pointed to the picture at the bottom of the page. "This dead girl!"

The one you killed? I only knew her for a few weeks.

I watched as Kaden translated only the last part of my answer.

"How many people saw you together?"

An old man gave us a ride from Tennessee to Greenville. We were picked up by a van full of college aged kids and dropped at the beach.

"How many?"

Three, two boys and a girl.

"And that's it?"

Them and the couple hundred people we passed on the beach that day.

I waited for Kaden to translate and watched Ray's face turn even redder.

"Fuck!" Ray threw the paper to the ground. "We've got to get rid of her, Kaden. This is serious now."

Kaden turned to face Ray, his back to me so I couldn't see what he was saying. Marshal sat on the couch, watching us like an episode from a TV drama. He saw me looking at him and signed 'hello' with a quick flip of his hand so his brother wouldn't notice. I shot him a small grin before resuming my frown.

Ray took a few steps toward Kaden and my attention returned to them.

"How much?" Ray looked like he was forcing himself to stay calm.

Kaden shrugged his shoulders and Ray glanced at me. His eyes danced over my body and face and a sudden understanding passed through his eyes. He took a few steps forward, pushing Kaden out of the way and staring at me like I was a piece of meat.

"I need you to tell me how much money is in your bank account."

Behind him, Kaden eyed me cautiously. Ray pulled my chin up.

"Don't look at him, look at me. Tell me how much is in your bank account?"

I froze. Did Kaden tell him the true amount or did he lie? And if he lied, by how much? What would happen if

Ray found out that Kaden or I had lied to him? He would probably take my money and then kill me for spite.

I held up my right hand. *1 – 5.*

"Fifteen?"

I nodded my head.

"Thousand?"

I nodded again.

Ray's massive body turned back to face Kaden.

Kaden shook his head, his eyes never leaving mine. "No, I didn't know."

Suddenly, Ray twirled me into his arms and pressed his chest against my back, his massive arms coiled around my body, holding me in place. I twitched and squirmed, trying to free myself, knowing I was helpless. Ray's arms squeezed me so tightly I felt my lungs being compressed against my ribs.

"I think we can get more. Just let her go."

Ray's fingers wrapped around my arms and crushed them.

"Because if we have her, we might as well try...You don't need that." Kaden looked like he desperately wanted to intervene but something held him back.

Ray's let go of my arm and reached for something out of the corner of my eye. Marshal handed him an object and I felt a cold blade pressed against my cheek. I closed my eyes and began to cry. The tip of the blade, sharp and menacing, made its way down my cheek and to my neck. My eyes flew open as it pressed into my skin.

"I could care less about her, but killing her will only get us thrown in jail." Kaden was pleading with Ray now but still not trying to physically stop him. I glanced at Marshal without moving my head. His hands were on the cushions, ready to push his body off the couch at a moment's notice if necessary, but his face was turned away.

"I know we can't half-ass anything now. If it doesn't work we'll take her to a bank, empty the account and you can kill her on the way to Mexico if you want."

The blade pushed a little harder and I felt a warm trickle of blood ooze down my neck. I took a deep breath, attempting to prevent myself from hyperventilaing. The pain was nothing compared to my fear. Ray was going to kill me if Kaden didn't tell him something he wanted to hear. I could do nothing to stop him. I couldn't see Ray's questions and I couldn't defend myself. I was completely in Kaden's hands.

"A phone call? Are you fucking serious? They'll trace that in minutes."

Who the hell did Ray want to call?

"Have her write a letter."

A letter? Was Kaden joking or was he getting desperate? But the blade moved from my neck and I relaxed slightly in Ray's arms. I felt his feet move behind mine as he pushed me toward the table and into a chair. I fell into the seat, my head spinning with confusion. Ray sat across from me. I wiped the blood from my neck with the back of my hand.

"You want to leave here, right?" Ray looked at me and set the kitchen knife on the table.

I blinked. Then nodded. What a thick question.

"Do you have any rich grandparents or uncles?"

I nodded again.

"I want you to write to one of them, whoever can get me the most money in the least amount of time. And make sure they can be discreet."

What do you want me to say?

Ray didn't even need Kaden to translate. Marshal set the paper and pen in front of me.

"Write whatever will get you out of here the fastest so I don't have to look at your fucking ugly face anymore! Tell them to wait for my instructions and if they say anything to anyone, I'll kill you." He pushed away from the table and stood up, leaving me to write my own ransom note.

Christopher,

I'm writing to beg your immediate help. The men who have taken me will be contacting you soon with instructions. Please give them whatever they want and don't ask questions or tell anyone what you are doing. I'm afraid they'll kill me. I'm afraid of never seeing you again.

Raleigh

I folded the letter, the blood from my fingers staining the edges of the paper. It was swiped from my hand and I turned to see Ray opening it and assessing my work. Kaden was reading over his shoulder and his eyes darted to mine as soon as he read the first name.

"Fine," Ray decided. "Give me the address and I'll drop it off tomorrow."

"Not from here, you won't." Kaden said behind him.

Ray spun around and pushed Kaden's shoulders, challenging him to question him again.

"You send that from around here and they'll be all over us. We need to drive it somewhere else, write our own letter, with our demands, and mail it from some random location."

If only Ray knew how much trouble he would get in if he actually sent that letter. His fingerprints were already all over it and his saliva would most likely be on the envelope. But the letter didn't matter. Kaden would never allow it to be sent, that much I knew. He was too smart and this was just a way of stalling.

I stood up to leave, ready to be away from the madness and Ray's anger. Kaden had been right, Ray didn't think, he only reacted. I prayed that he wouldn't stop to think before I was gone. I stepped around the two men, still arguing about something, when I felt Ray's rough fingers grab my arm. I turned to face him, ready to see whatever it was he had to say to me, but he didn't speak. His spare hand flew through the air and hit me across my cheek, knocking me to the ground with one blow.

My head spun and my vision blurred. I stayed on the ground for what seemed like minutes, trying to regain my focus. No hands came to help me to my feet, no arms wrapped around me protectively. I didn't know what I had done to deserve that, nor did I care. As the tears started to pour from my eyes, I finally stood up and staggered to the basement door.

For the first time since I had been in this house, my mattress and sheets were a welcoming sight. I climbed under their caring shield, turned onto my side, curling my legs to my chest and closing my eyes. The tears fell freely onto my pillow.

Hours passed and I didn't move. My bed offered the only comfort I had left and I was growing accustomed to its hard and scratchy embrace. But something disturbed my peace. I felt the mattress tremble as someone climbed on behind me and I opened my eyes, only partly wanting to see who it was. The lights had been turned off but as soon as he touched me, I knew and was not afraid. The sheets were pulled up and away from me as I felt Kaden's body slide behind mine. His arm wrapped around my waist, pulling me as close as I would go, and then rested around my ribs. The other hand was softly stroking my hair onto the mattress and his lips left a single kiss on the back of my neck.

I closed my eyes again and fell asleep.

Chapter 10

I woke up to the dull light of the basement. My head throbbed. Did Kaden really come to my bed or had it been a dream? It had seemed real. I turned over and inhaled deeply, hoping his scent still lingered. I wasn't disappointed. The mattress still held the subtle aroma of soap and cinnamon. I hadn't figured out why he smelled of cinnamon, but I loved the scent. It reminded me of my mother and the holidays we spent in London.

I climbed out of bed, my head feeling as if it had been left in a vice overnight. My feet dragged as I slumped over to my clothes. Kaden still expected me to wear his oversized shirts every day. I had collected half a dozen or so which I kept folded next to my bed. I washed them in the sink along with my underwear. Needless to say, I had grown accustomed to wearing stiff undergarments and t-shirts. My jeans were another story completely. By now, they were starting to get baggy and fell below my hip bones. Soon I would have to start rolling them at the waist to keep them up.

But none of this really bothered me. I was rarely hungry anymore and was actually grateful I had some place to wash my belongings. I dressed as quickly as my head would allow, stripping off my t-shirt before clasping my bra and choosing a clean top. My hair was pushed from my eyes and twirled to one shoulder.

Once dressed, I peered up the stairs. The door had been left open and I could see bright sunlight streaming in from the windows. The term cabin-fever had never been of much use in my vocabulary until now. Climbing the stairs, I could see Kaden in the living room waiting for me. His green eyes looked gentle in the bright light and his fingers were casually hooked through his belt loops, instead of crossed in front of his chest in his usual defensive stance.

He watched me climb the last of the stairs and waited until I was standing in front of him to speak. "How's your head?" He reached up and brushed a stray curl behind my ear.

"It hurts."

Kaden nodded, his hand lingering near my jaw. "Have some breakfast, it should help." He motioned for me to sit at the table and I obeyed, cradling my head in my hands as I slumped into the chair. His kindness was doing little to help my headache. His mood swings kept me wondering what he was really thinking and I was beginning to believe he was mentally unstable. Or just possibly very conflicted. Conflicted over what was the true mystery. In my mind, the decision was simple: take the money that was offered and get the hell out of the States. But Kaden had said he needed more time, which meant he was planning something larger.

He set a plate of scrambled eggs and bacon in front of me and then took a seat across the table. I stared at the food, enjoying the familiar yet nearly forgotten scent, and slowly reached for the fork which was teetering on the edge of the plate. Casually, I glanced up at Kaden, an unwanted smile starting to creep over my face as my gratitude forged its way through my wall of defense. Tears flooded my eyes. It felt as if I had been given the best gift of my life.

"Are you about to cry over eggs?" Kaden grinned at me.

A slight sob escaped in the form of a laugh as I tried to blink back the tears. "Yes," I answered, unashamed of my emotions.

"I'm not that bad of a cook, I promise."

I laughed again and dug my fork into the fluffy scramble. After that first taste, my stomach ached for more. But I took my time, savoring each bite. Kaden watched me eat, a smile on his face the entire time. But half way through, I was finished, unable to stomach anymore. I gently set my fork back on my plate and sat back in my chair, perfectly satisfied for the first time in over a month.

Kaden stood up and picked up my half empty plate. His free hand gently turned my face up to his. "I want you to be ready in ten minutes."

"For what?"

His fingers spread over my jaw and fanned down my neck; his eyes swept over my body. But he didn't speak. I gulped as he turned away toward the kitchen.

"For what?" I repeated, but he didn't answer.

Even though I was happy to stay in my chair and linger in my new found contentment, yesterday's interaction with Kaden still had me scared. I didn't want to push him to such extremes again, but as I walked up the stairs to the bathroom and stripped off my clothes for a quick shower, I found myself wondering what it would be like to make love to Kaden; to have him gently and caringly take his time with me, exploring and learning my body, instead of using me and throwing me aside.

When I returned downstairs, my hair still damp from the shower, Kaden was waiting for me at the front door. The door stood wide open, allowing the warm October breeze to flow through the living room. I stopped in my tracks, afraid of what awaited outside. Freedom was unlikely, death a higher possibility. Even though I was rarely comfortable inside the house, the outside was now unknown - and the unknown scared me.

Kaden could see my trepidation and raised his hand, gesturing for me to come closer. "Come on. We're just going for a walk."

"Why?" My defensive question caused his lips to twitch at the corners.

"Because I thought you would enjoy it."

I looked at the brilliant light of the outdoors. I could smell the trees and the clean fragrance of the nature; it was calling to me. But then I glanced at the door to the basement. I could walk down those stairs and be alone, away from Kaden and his viciously inconsistent behavior. I remembered how yellow my skin had looked in the mirror just a few moments before. My hair had lost its shine, dark circles had formed under my eyes.

I took a few hesitant steps forward, brushing past Kaden and into the light. I inhaled through my nose and mouth, smelling and tasting the clean air that surrounded me like an embrace from a long lost friend. I would have been happy to stay on the front stoop of the house but Kaden appeared beside me, a blanket under one arm, and motioned for us to venture further. Again, he offered his hand, and again I refused to take it. Part of him looked sad by the refusal, part of him looked infuriated by it, but he didn't let either side win.

Kaden walked in front of me for nearly half an hour. I constantly stopped to look up at the sky or marvel at the brilliant autumn colors. I felt his hand pulling at my elbow if I paused for too long, hurrying me along as if we had some sort of pressing appointment. The thought that he would be taking me far away from the house only to kill me didn't pass my mind until I saw our destination. The path opened to a small lake, blue and sparkling with the reflection of the morning sky. Kaden walked to a small dock where a paddle boat was bobbing up and down in the gentle tide. Was he going to drown me? Leave me tied to a brick at the bottom of the lake? But he walked a few steps onto the dock and spread the blanket out, lying down and stretching his arms wide.

I looked around, a sudden urge to run had taken hold of me. Here, where there was so much to run through, so much to hide behind, I could easily get lost in the woods. He would hear me running, no doubt, for I had no idea how much noise my footsteps would make. And what would he do to me if I ran? No, the safest option was to convince him to accept the money and set me free, or wait until my father realized I was missing. Although, the amount of time it would take for both or either of those events to occur could be infinite.

I moved closer to the dock and eventually joined Kaden on the blanket. I imitated his movements, lying on my back, closing my eyes, and stretching my arms. The warm air and the bright sun felt incredible against my sallow skin. On days like these, back home in Delaware, I would be on the beach, lying in a bikini with a good novel or chatting with my best friends. But now I was lying on a rickety dock in baggy jeans and a man's t-shirt; my only company was my kidnapper.

I opened my eyes and I felt Kaden's fingers on my neck, tracing the curve of my shoulder and the hollow area above my collar bone.

"Stop," I said turning my head toward him. He had rolled onto his side, his elbow next to my shoulder, his head in his hand.

He shook his head and I frowned, knowing it would be useless to fight. His eyes and skin were practically glowing in the sunlight, his hair falling to the side of his face above his brow. I studied his face, his high cheekbones, his strong jaw and chin, and wondered what about this man had so captivated me. I was terrified of him but at the same time wanted him to desire me. I wanted him to care for me and protect me.

Kaden pushed himself closer, keeping his hand on my shoulder. His eyes were peaceful and not intimidating so I wasn't at all scared when he bent his head down and kissed the small wound Ray's knife had cut on my neck.

He stared into my eyes. His fingers glided over my collar bone.

"Why are you doing this?" I asked.

"Doing what?" He looked at my lips as he spoke.

"Why are you being nice to me?"

His mouth stretched into a smile. "I'm not a bad person, Raleigh. I've just done some fucked up things lately."

I raised my eyebrows at his understatement. "So now you're feeling guilty for what you've done? Are you trying to make it up to me, because, believe me, that's never going to happen."

Kaden lay there for a minute without moving his lips, just staring at me. Finally he spoke, "I'm not trying to atone for my actions because I don't regret anything I've done. I'm learning to live with the decisions I've made and am making the best of them."

With that I sat up and pushed his hand away. "And what about me, Kaden? I'm not a bad person either but I've been forced to live with your decisions. I have no say in any of this, no hint or insinuation about what's going to happen to me. I live, day to day, wondering if you're going to speak to me, kill me, or worse."

Kaden didn't sit up, allowing me, for once, to look down on him. "I agree, it's not fair to you. But what happened yesterday isn't worse than death. I know you know that."

"You don't know how I feel. You don't know how terrifying and humiliating this is."

"I don't want you to be scared when you're with me," Kaden said, sitting up and reaching for my hand. "You never need to be scared."

"You say that, but look at what you've done to me!"

"Let me explain it to you, then." I could tell he was getting upset. His eyes started to squint and his lips pressed tightly together. "When you and I are alone, when Ray and Marshal are out of the house, you belong to me."

I pulled my hand away, shocked by his words. I would never belong to anyone, especially Kaden. "What about that statement wouldn't scare me?"

"Just listen to me." He put two hands on my thighs to keep me from moving. "What I meant was, just let me finish."

I glared at him. It was a simple and common mistake to make. It had happened with my closest of friends and we always laughed about it. But Kaden had felt some remorse for his slip of tongue and I wasn't about to comfort him over it.

"I want you with me all the time, Raleigh. I meant what I said that night, about not being able to put you out of my mind. Ever since I kissed you, I've wanted nothing more than to be with you. I thought that I would be able to forget about you, let you waste away down in the basement until I no longer recognized you. But then yesterday you made me so angry that I lost all sense of self control and now it's too late. I've had you once and I need you again. I don't know if I will ever stop needing to touch you or wanting to feel you against me."

I turned away from him, not caring if he had anything more to say. Everything surrounding me was tranquil and serene but I felt like a ticking time bomb, ready to explode. The water gently lapped against the rocky shore. The trees displayed their fall colors, hardening for the rough winter that lay ahead. The blue sky was flawlessly clear. How could things remain so beautiful in the outside world when my entire existence had just been claimed by a man who was little more than a stranger?

I felt my body start to shake. I blinked away a few tears and tried to compose myself. Kaden's strong arms pulled me close to his hard chest, wrapping around me securely.

It wouldn't be that bad, would it, allowing Kaden absolute control over me? In some sick and twisted way, he seemed to care about me, enough to let me cry on his shoulder, at least. No, things could be worse. All three of the men could divide ownership of me, and at least one of them wasn't as kind as Kaden proved he could sometimes be.

So I made up my mind and lifted my head to Kaden's. As soon as our eyes met, I spoke. "I'm yours, on one condition."

A quick raise of one eyebrow told me I had surprised him. "What's that?"

I knew he wasn't going to allow me to name my own terms, but this was more of a favor than anything else. "I'm not strong enough to stop you from taking what you want. But I'm also not strong enough to live with the abuse of being thrown aside when you're finished. All I ask is that when you're done, don't dismiss me like an afterthought. Let me stay for a moment so I can at least pretend that everything is going to be all right."

His eyes softened again and he nodded. His hands gently lowered me back to the blanket and he positioned himself over me. "You will never feel alone again," he said before brushing his lips against mine. His kiss was passionate and gentle but I sensed the conflict in him. He was worried I would change my mind, start to fight him off. I could tell how badly he wanted me.

He kissed me for what seemed like hours that day, slowly stripping away not only layers of my clothes but of my defensive wall as well. The noon sun found us lying side by side, me in nothing but my bra and panties, Kaden in only his boxers, our eyes closed in the resigned comfort of our new understanding.

Chapter 11

"Raleigh, Darling, are you awake?" My mother's voice sounded like a distant whisper. I opened my eyes and realized she was standing over my bed. I was too uncomfortable to speak or to move, so I blinked at her from behind my heavy eyes.

"How are you feeling today?" She asked, knowing very well that I wasn't going to respond.

"You look much better," she continued, wiping the perspiration from my clammy face.

I looked across the room as she turned her head. My father had entered the room, but I hadn't heard him. I saw his lips moving as he spoke to my mother but I couldn't hear the words. His face looked worn and his eyes looked tired. His head nodded towards the door and I felt my mother stand up. I watched her walk across the room and place a hand on my father's arm. But he wouldn't look at her. His eyes moved to my bed and I blinked under his stare. I had never seen him act so cold.

My mother left when my father didn't acknowledge her, hanging her head and wiping away tears. As the door closed, my father walked slowly to my bed, his heavy eyes now filled with sadness and worry.

I started to shiver as a cold wave passed over my body. My father looked at me helplessly and put a hand over his mouth as he choked back a sob. My body started

*to shake uncontrollably and my eyes closed in response
to the terrifying tremors.*

"Raleigh?" I heard my father say.

"Raleigh, wake up! Raleigh!"

My eyes opened and I blinked at the sunlight. I could feel Kaden's lips on my ribs and looked down to see his dark hair just below the curve of my breast. He must have felt me move for he looked up and smiled.

"I didn't want to wake you, but you're starting to turn pink."

I looked down and saw that indeed my chest and belly were starting to redden in the afternoon sun. I pushed myself onto my elbows and looked at Kaden, his head resting nonchalantly on my lower abdomen, resisting an urge to reach up and run my fingers through his unruly black hair.

He stared back for a moment, a casual smile still on his face. His lips returned to my skin. He kissed down my stomach and paused before reaching up and slipping a finger under the elastic band of my panties. Defensively, I crossed my legs and sat up, moving my hips away from his face. His head swung in defeat just above my knees before he sat up and reached for his shirt.

I watched for only a second as he pulled the fabric over his head and covered the muscles of his shoulders and stomach. I quickly followed suit, reaching for my clothes and pulling them on. Kaden wasted no time lifting the blanket off the dock before throwing it over his shoulder and walking back toward the trees. I wasn't eager to leave the serenity of the lake, but I wasn't in a position to demand or ask for anything. Kaden stopped at the beginning of the path and turned to face me.

"Hold my hand," he said as he stretched his arm toward me.

I took a few steps and reached for it, lightly placing my palm against his. His fingers closed around mine as he started walking again, pulling me behind him. I had to quicken my step to keep up with him, his legs, much longer than mine, as we tread across the uneven ground.

The shingled roof come into view and I craned my neck to see the driveway. It was empty, and I sighed in relief. I hadn't seen Ray's car since the morning they brought me to the house. I imagined they had already fixed the damage, probably claiming they had hit a deer instead of two women.

Kaden let go of my hand, bounded up to the front door and unlocked it. I took one last look at the afternoon sky before returning to my prison. The oranges and yellows of the changing leaves contrasted brilliantly with the blue sky. Waving gently in the breeze, the limbs of the trees seemed to be dancing together, perhaps celebrating their last warm day before the bitter cold of winter froze them to their core. I closed my eyes and tried to imprint the image into my head. This was ever so much nicer than staring at dust falling from ceiling rafters. Inhaling a last breath of fresh air, I opened my eyes and walked through the open door, passing Kaden as I stepped inside. I was halfway across the living room when I felt his grip on my elbow.

"I'd like you to come upstairs with me," he said as I turned to face him.

I eyed the front door. "What about Ray and Marshal? Won't they be back soon?"

Kaden shook his head and pulled me gently toward him as a smile crept over his face. "They are on their way to Virginia to mail your letter and won't be back until tomorrow morning. At the earliest," he added with a tilt of his cocky head.

"Where are you mailing it to? 1600 Pennsylvania Avenue?"

Kaden's smile faded and he glared at me. "Clever, but not quite. You'd be surprised just how easy it is to obtain a PO Box over the Internet. Your letter is on its way to Dover, and it will be waiting there until I can no longer afford the yearly payments."

I wasn't surprised to hear this. While incredibly incriminating if discovered, Kaden's diversion would buy him some time.

"Where do they usually go during the day?" I asked, wanting to change the subject.

"Why do you care?"

"Just curious, I guess."

I could see him debating whether or not he wanted to answer me and finally he gave in. "They're at work."

"Where?"

"The docks," he answered quickly.

"Why don't you work?" I knew I was letting my curiosity get the better of me but I couldn't stop myself.

"I work from here." He pushed his hair out of his eyes and gave me an exasperated look.

"Doing what?"

"I'm done with the twenty questions, Raleigh," he snapped. "We're going upstairs so we can finish what you didn't even let me start back at the lake."

I took a deep breath, knowing that what he wanted was inevitable. His hand was still on my elbow as I reached for his arm, lightly squeezing his bicep beneath his shirt.

"Okay," I answered, forcing a smile.

He seemed shocked at my acceptance and nodded slightly before leading me up the stairs and to his bedroom. I glanced at the doorframe on my way in, noting the marks on the wood from my fingernails only a day earlier. Things seemed so different now. I knew I wasn't going upstairs willingly, but I wasn't being dragged, kicking and screaming, either.

I stepped inside his room and looked around, something I hadn't thought or wanted to do the last time I occupied this space. The walls were painted a light shade of grey, very similar to the color of my eyes. There were no pictures on the walls but a blue curtain adorned the windows opposite the door and added some depth to the room. His bed was exactly how I had left it the day before, the blue comforter strewn to the side, the pillows carelessly thrown about. A black dresser stood alone against the wall next to the closet, a deck of cards and notebook were the only things resting on it. From across the bed, I could see his nightstand with only a desk lamp, a book, and an empty glass.

Walking around to the nightstand, trying to pretend that I wasn't shaking with fear, I picked up the thick book. *Vingt Mille Lieues Sous Les Mers.* I smiled at the cover. It had been one of my favorite books as a child, in English and abridged, of course. I held it in my hand and traced the perforated cover with my fingers.

I was very nearly ready to put it down when I felt Kaden's hand wrap around my stomach from behind, pulling me flush against his body. His other hand gently took the book and returned it to the nightstand.

"You can ask me about it later," he said after he had turned me to face him. His eyes held mine as he softly stoked my cheek. I stared up at him. His face looked so kind and gentle, I was almost able to forget where I was. Hesitantly, I moved my hand to his chest, lightly tracing the muscles I knew were hiding beneath his clothing. His pupils flared with pleasure and he bent down to kiss me. His lips were so soft that I gave into the kiss completely, knowing it would only encourage him, but hoping it would speed things along and get it over quickly.

His kiss became stronger and his hands gripped the fabric of my shirt. It wasn't until a slight moan escaped my throat that he pushed us onto the bed, falling on top of me and straddling my legs. He kissed me again as he worked the t-shirt up my stomach and over my chest. Our lips broke apart. He sat up and pulled my top off. His shirt was next and I ran my eyes over his impeccable physique. He pushed himself off the bed, grabbing my hips and swinging my legs so they were dangling from the edge of the mattress. His fingers worked slowly to unbutton my jeans, his knuckle brushing against my panties as he lowered it.

His hand ran over my sides and stomach and then his fingers walked up each of my ribs, making sure to touch each protruding bone. Slowly, he lowered his lips to my stomach, kissing my bellybutton then following his fingers to kiss each of my ribs.

I hated this. I hated that I wanted him. I hated that what he was doing was driving me insane. So I held my breath, fearing that if I inhaled, it would bring us closer together. But that didn't stop a whimper, or it could have been a moan, from escaping my lips. He kissed me lightly at my neck and I felt his hot breath on my jaw. I closed my eyes, knowing he was going to kiss me again. My head was swimming with doubt, yearning, frustration, lust, and fear. But he kissed me passionately, like we were lovers, like I belonged to him and him to me.

His hands explored my skin as he kissed me, but mine stayed firmly pressed to the bed. I had not wanted this to happen again, but now that he had started, I didn't want him to stop and it was becoming increasingly difficult to restrain myself. I wanted to reach up and touch his face, run my fingers across his back and through his dark hair, but I couldn't allow myself to do so. It was too dangerous, and I was already in peril of losing my better judgment when it came to Kaden.

But, as if he knew what I was thinking, one of his strong hands wrapped around my wrist and forced my hand to his side. He pressed my fingers firmly into his skin, still kissing me, and only released my hand when he knew I understood what he wanted. His kiss became more demanding and his hand ran down my side and across my hip. That's when I knew there was no turning back. Kaden would have what he wanted and I would be left with the residual effects of the pleasure, nothing more, nothing less.

Kaden's touch spread the ache in my heart throughout my entire body. I needed the physical release as much as the emotional one. I waited, almost impatiently, for him to begin yet he was taking his time, teasing me and allowing my anticipation to grow. This was so different from the last time we were together.

Did he want me to battle him off? Was he giving me time to think about it? I knew I wouldn't be able to last much longer but I also knew that Kaden was too skilled at what he was doing for me to put up a fight. So I gave in, my breathing becoming faster, my eyes closing and my fingers digging into his back.

My quivering body was pushed across the bed and Kaden rested himself between my legs. I felt his fingers on my face, then a light touch brushed my eyelid and rubbed my temple. Opening my eyes to see Kaden's face above mine caused me to blush with embarrassment and turn my head. But his hand was quick to correct my action, turning my face gently back toward his.

"I want you to look at me. Don't imagine you are anywhere else but here with me." His eyes were serious as he spoke so I nodded in understanding. "Your enjoyment only adds to my pleasure, but don't forget that I'm forcing you to do this."

I nodded again although his statement confused me. His arms were like steel bars on either side of my shoulders, the muscles in his arms flexing to hold him up and protect me from the weight of his body. I let him work, adjusting nearly instinctively to meet his needs. I could feel all of him, his chest brushing against mine, the sweat on his skin, the muscles of his back, his full lips as he kissed me.

But I had to remind myself that I shouldn't be enjoying. this. I had to remind myself that I shouldn't be helping him; I should be wanting this act to be over and done with. But, I would have been lying. "Kaden," I said between moans, knowing it would only encourage him. His mouth found my neck; his movements became more erratic.

"Kaden!" I screamed. I could feel him reaching his climax, his teeth biting down on my skin. He collapsed on top of me, his chest crushing mine with each full breath he took. My hands lingered on his back. His warm breath on my shoulder became steady before he raised his head to look at me. He eyes held so much emotion, so much passion, that I melted right there on the bed. I could see that what we had done hadn't been just an act for him. He hadn't been just going through the motions. Kaden hadn't just fucked me; we didn't have sex. No, Kaden had made love to me. It had been more than physically intimate; he had taken his time, explored everything about me, and made me want to please him just as much as he was pleasing me.

I knew it was wrong. I knew it would only lead to further confusion and emotional distress, but I could no longer deny what I felt. My fingers traced his spine up to his neck before running through his soft hair. I lifted my head hesitantly and stopped just short of his lips, waiting to see if he would pull away. When he didn't move, I found the courage to touch his lips with mine. I gave him a soft kiss then rested my head back on the mattress.

His eyes were a mixture of full of pleasure and guilt. "What was that for?"

I shook my head, unable to give him an honest answer. "Am I not allowed to kiss you?"

"You shouldn't want to," he replied.

"If it makes you upset, I won't do it again," I promised, more embarrassed than hurt. I didn't want my face to betray how amazing he still felt above me.

He waited a moment, but soon turned my face back to his with a gentle hand. "The only thing that upsets me is knowing that our time together is limited. You can kiss me whenever you like."

I didn't smile at this. I didn't feel like he had conceded anything. Of course our time was limited. He had known that from the start. Clearly, he was stalling, prolonging the inevitable for his pleasure as well as the chance to make a considerable amount of money.

Kaden smiled, running his fingers from my chin to my cheek and down my neck.

"I didn't hurt you, did I?"

"I may be sore tomorrow." I paused, unsure if I wanted to massage his ego with what he would surely take to be a compliment. "You're...you're not exactly what I'm used to."

He smiled again but didn't look cocky this time. "Yes, I can feel that." He moved slowly in and out a few times, taking his time to let me feel every inch of him. I couldn't remember the last time anything had felt so good.

I was prepared to have him take me again, ready to be thrown back into the heat of our undeniable lust for one another, but he stopped.

"I was talking about your neck." He smiled at me as I took a deep breath.

"You bit me!" I suddenly remembered, feigning anger at what he had done.

Kaden laughed and rolled away, denying me the pleasure of a second round. With one strong arm, he pulled me on top of him so my torso was resting on his chest and my face was close to his.

"It was the way you said my name," he reminded me, closing his eyes.

I knew what I had done and I couldn't deny it. I pulled a hand from under my body and placed it gently on his chest. Gradually, I moved it up his body until my fingers were laying flat against the bottom of his throat, surrounding his Adam's apple and filling the hollow of his neck.

"Can you say my name?" I asked.

Kaden's eyes remained closed and he didn't move. I was sure he had heard me but I wasn't ready to give up.

"Please? I'd really like to feel you say it."

He took a couple deep breaths, his lips pressed tightly together, but eventually he opened his eyes. His free hand reached up for mine and pressed my fingers hard against his neck.

"Raleigh."

I smiled after he had pushed my hand away from his throat. I could still feel the vibrations in my fingers. His voice had felt scratchy and deep against my fingers, as if it came from his soul instead of his larynx.

My eyes closed, suddenly heavy and exhausted. I felt Kaden turn onto his side and pull me close to his warm skin. His fingers ran slowly up and down my arm a few times before falling across my chest. Our breathing moved into sync as we both fell asleep.

Chapter 12

I opened my eyes to see the sun setting behind the trees. Warm light filled the room and I smiled, rolling onto my back and stretching my arms above my head. Suddenly, a strong hand gripped my wrists and pinned them to the headboard of the bed. I let out a small cry of shock before seeing Kaden's face sweep in above mine. He smiled down at me before switching to his scowl.

"Did I scare you?"

"Yes," I answered, very aware that I was still naked under the sheets.

"Are you hungry?" he asked, releasing my hands and kneeling beside me.

I had to think about it. I even tried to find the sensation inside my stomach and magnify it, but it was no use. "No," I finally answered.

Kaden frowned. "Well, I've made dinner so you're going to join me."

"All right," I smiled, sensing his frustration but finding it amusing that he had to command me to join him for a meal.

"You should get dressed," he added. "But not too dressed. You're too beautiful to be covered up."

He stood up and left before I could react. I watched him walk out of the room, his khaki shorts and dark blue t-shirt hiding what I already missed, and I allowed, for the second time that day, a genuine smile to come to my face. Beautiful? I had never been called beautiful before. Pretty, yes. Hot? Only once by a drunk college kid at a bar. But never beautiful.

I sat up and let the sheets fall to my waist before kicking them off and examining myself. Large, dark freckles blemished my pale skin. My breasts were full and too large for my body, my waist sloped sharply between my ribs and hips, something my mother used to call an hourglass figure but what I considered a headache. I could never find clothes that fit. My hips flared and my legs, which were once toned and shapely, now looked skinny and frail. I couldn't understand what Kaden found beautiful about me, but I had spent too many hours thinking about him to care.

I stepped out of the bed, found my underwear on the ground and slipped them on. Kaden's closet door had been left open so I walked over and ran my fingers over the clothes hanging inside. There were very few items, mostly collared shirts, but a black suit hanging to one side caught my eye. The fabric looked and felt expensive. The hanger was wood and held the shape of the jacket. The more time I spent with Kaden, the more of an enigma he became. Why did he need an expensive suit? Why was he reading *Twenty Thousand Leagues Under the Sea* in French?

I pulled a white collared shirt from the hanger and buttoned it just enough to cover my naked chest. The shirt hung to my middle thighs and I held my head high as I walked down the stairs, determined to learn more about this man who held my body and heart in his hand.

Kaden was in the kitchen, standing above the stove, pushing something around in a frying pan. It smelled amazing, like cinnamon and vanilla, not exactly scents I associated with dinner, but delicious, nonetheless. I pulled out a chair and sat, watching the way his shoulder muscles moved under his t-shirt. He grabbed two plates from the counter and dished whatever he was cooking.

Kaden turned toward me and I could tell he was trying to suppress a smile.

"That's my favorite shirt you're wearing, Blondie," he said, setting my plate down.

"Can I borrow it for a few hours?" I asked, trying to play coy.

"If it will smell like you the next time I wear it, then of course you can borrow it." I blushed as he bent down and kissed my head. Six weeks ago, I would have never imagined my face would be red from anything but crying or screaming.

I finally looked down at my food. French toast. I glanced at Kaden to help ease my confusion.

"I can only make breakfast food," he said with a shrug.

"That explains why you always smell like cinnamon." I smiled at him before picking up my fork and cutting into the toast. It wasn't anything special, just the basic recipe, but something about it tasted unique. Maybe it was because I hadn't tasted bread in so long. Maybe it was because Kaden had made it for me.

I put my fork down halfway through my first piece, a sharp pain stabbing at my stomach, and pushed my plate away. I could see Kaden from the other side of the table giving me a strange look, but I didn't want to meet his gaze. I knew there would be questions and I knew I would only blame him for my inability to finish a piece of toast. But I didn't want to upset him; I didn't want to upset myself, so I casually looked around the room. The appliances were in better condition, thanks to my cleaning, and the dishes had recently been done so the sink was nearly empty. There was nothing that could be done about the dingy yellow wallpaper and the stained linoleum floor.

I remembered one of the first days I had spent in this kitchen. I had found it so bizarre there were no windows or a back door. It had felt as if this house was designed to hold me prisoner, but now, sitting with Kaden, the room didn't give me the same feeling. I felt almost giddy occupying the same space as him.

I smiled at the pleasant change in events. Kaden stepped in front of me.

"Are you finished?"

I nodded.

"You should eat more," he said, pushing my plate back in front of me.

"I can't," I admitted. "It hurts."

Kaden glared at me and picked up my plate, stomped over to the garbage bin and tossed the remaining food carelessly inside. The plate was thrown into the sink and I watched as it shattered against the porcelain edges.

"I'm sorry," I stared at him in shock, slightly confused and completely scared of the way he was acting.

"Why are you apologizing?" he asked, folding his arms across his chest and leaning against the counter.

I shook my head. "You seem upset. I didn't mean to..."

"Of course I'm upset! You're practically starving to death and it's mostly my fault!"

"It will get better," I tried to reason with him although his neck was tense and a large vein had appeared on his forehead. "It may just take some time. I haven't been eating very much for the past..."

"Quit trying to make me feel better about this." Kaden took a few large steps in my direction and knelt by my chair so he was at eye level with me. Why was I trying to make him feel better about my situation? It was mostly his fault, that much was true. But I knew that I wanted to remain inside the fantasy Kaden and I had created. I was prepared to do anything to keep the fantasy alive, even if it meant justifying a kidnapper's cruel and demeaning ways of inflicting dominance.

"You aren't responsible for any of this and my feelings for you are making my culpability in this situation all the more apparent." He wasn't going to let this go. Was it possible that he was truly conflicted? Did he have knots in his stomach caused by guilt? Did they feel like the knots in mine caused by the anxiety of the unknown? Perhaps he had spent sleepless nights pondering what the ramifications of his actions were going to be; how he had potentially ruined the lives of his two friends; how he had potentially ruined the life of a stranger and taken the life of her companion?

He seemed to have calmed down but then he grabbed my hands and held them so tightly I was afraid he would crush the bones. "I don't want you to be scared of me, Raleigh. Honestly, I don't." But isn't that what he wanted? Isn't that why I had been denied so much for so long?

"What do you want, then? Because, honestly, I'm terrified of you."

His eyes looked hurt by my words but his hands loosened their grip. "What about me terrifies you?"

I took a deep breath. Where to begin? "I'm scared of your temper. I'm scared of your friends. I'm scared of dying. I'm scared that I'm allowing myself to feel something that isn't real. I'm scared that you'll change your mind and not want me anymore." There, I said it.

Kaden smiled at my confession. "The second I don't want you anymore, you are free to leave."

I'm scared that day will never come, I thought to myself, though I didn't say it out loud. Kaden enjoyed his dominance over me and I had learned to play his affection. There was no reason to disturb that delicate balance now.

Kaden's placed his hands on my bare knees, slowly rubbing up and down my thighs. I knew what he wanted, I could tell by the lusty look in his emerald eyes, but since he had promised me my freedom once he was done with me, I wasn't going to give in that easily.

"Tell me what you do, Kaden," I said as he worked his way higher up my leg.

He eyed me with a knowing look that I remembered from my first day here.

"I translate books and manuscripts."

"From French to English or English to French?"

"French to English. You get five more questions."

"I want ten."

"Seven."

"Fine. Where did you learn French?"

"My Dad is French Algerian, I grew up in Paris."

"But you don't have an accent."

"That's not a question." He smiled back at me and then stood up, holding his hand out. I allowed him to lead me into the living room and sat down on the couch.

"It's an observation. I can tell from the way your lips and tongue move when you speak. You would sound American to anyone else."

"You can tell that from reading my lips?"

I nodded.

"All right, I'll give you this one for free because that's impressive. My mom is American and I grew up speaking French and American English, as my dad calls it."

"Where are your parents now?"

"Morocco."

"How did you end up here?" None of these questions clarified anything for me.

"I went to college in Charleston, then moved up here to live with Ray."

Right. Ray. "How do you know him?"

Kaden shifted in his seat, apparently a bit uneasy at my question. "I used to spend the summers with Ray and his family at their beach house. Our mothers were best friends."

I frowned. That seemed like a perfectly normal explanation but he had seemed so uncomfortable answering it. I was curious but didn't want to push that subject. Not talking about Ray made everything a lot easier.

"Why do you know sign language?"

"My grandfather on my mother's side was deaf. You have two more questions."

I smiled, thinking hard about the last inquiries. Nothing but casual, first-date type questions came to mind.

"How old are you?"

"Thirty one."

"And...why are you reading *Twenty Thousand Leagues Under the Sea?* They've already translated that book."

"I just like reading it."

I leaned back against the cushions. I hadn't learned much, but it was a start.

"My turn," he said.

"Fine. You get seven questions."

"Why were you hitchhiking in North Carolina?"

"I didn't want to take the job my father offered me so I told him I was going to Europe for a few months and started hitching rides from the airport. I wasn't going anywhere in particular."

"Weren't you scared? Isn't hitchhiking a little dangerous for a young woman?"

"I guess it proved to be rather perilous, didn't it?"

Kaden raised an eyebrow at my remark but kept going. "What did you study in school?"

"Political Science and Economics."

"Masters Degree?"

"PhD."

His eyebrow rose again and I countered with a crooked smile.

"What do you want to do with the rest of your life?"

Now it was my turn to shift uncomfortably. How long was the rest of my life going to be? Was his question hypothetical or was he really intending to collect the money and let me leave?

"I don't know."

"That's not an answer."

I stared at his gorgeous green eyes. They were unwavering, unrelenting, so I chose to answer the question in terms of how my life used to be.

"I stayed in school as long as I could, finishing everything my father agreed to pay for. Now I have absolutely no desire to go into politics or some think-tank in Washington. So, in all honesty, I really don't know."

"So you ran away. That's an observation, not a question," he added quickly.

I nodded, angered that he was able to discover so much about me with his seven questions and I hadn't even thought to ask him his full name. Kaden moved closer to me on the couch, pulling my legs over his lap and twirling one of the buttons on my shirt with his free hand.

"Will you go with me to the lake again tomorrow?"

It was more of an invitation, really.

"Yes," I answered, surprised that I felt shy answering.

"Last question," Kaden started. "Can I please have my shirt back?" His hand reached under his white shirt and skimmed along my side until his thumb rested at the bottom of my breast. His touch was like a drug, instantly masking my anxiety and breaking down my inhibitions.

"What? This shirt?" I popped the collar and pulled it tight around my neck.

Kaden nodded as he gently caressed my skin.

"No," I finally decided. "I like it and it looks good on me."

"It does look good on you. But I'll be needing it back right now," he said as his other hand disappeared under the fabric and made its way up my ribs. He was holding me so he knew I couldn't move, but his grip wasn't tight.

I bit my lip and shook my head. "No. I'm keeping it."

He tilted his head in defiance and lowered his face towards mine. Our lips brushed but he didn't kiss me. He mouth hovered above mine for what seemed like an eternity.

"You'll have to rip it from me," I whispered against his lips when I could take no more of his teasing.

His mouth instantly crushed mine in a fiery kiss. His hands left my chest and guided my arms around his neck, then helped wrap my legs around his waist. He stood up with me in his arms, acting as if I weighed nothing at all, and carried me upstairs, both of us smiling the entire way to the bedroom.

Chapter 13

"Have you ever been in love, Raleigh?" Julie was sitting in the sand, her toes and fingers buried beneath the warm surface. Her face looked solemn, something I wasn't used to seeing from such an animated woman.

"I thought I was, once." I didn't know much about her even though for the past couple of weeks we had gotten along incredibly well.

"What happened?"

"He left me for another girl. We were twelve."

Julie laughed and her mood lightened. "I've been in love too many times. Probably enough for the both of us."

"What happened?"

"With which one?"

"The last one, I guess."

She sighed and dug her toes deeper into the sand. "He found out some things about my past that he didn't agree with. He left me just a few weeks before I met you."

"What did he find out?" I knew I was prying but she wouldn't have brought it up if she didn't want to talk about it.

"That I have a child."

I stared at her, stunned.

"She lives with her father in Atlanta. The court said I wasn't fit to raise a child and gave him full custody."

"Are you on your way to see her?"

Julie nodded and stared into the sand. I could tell she was speaking but I couldn't see her lips.

"Julie, I can't..."

"Sorry," she smiled and looked up at me. "It's just a little shameful, not being able to raise your own daughter."

"But you're going to see her; you can make a new start. I think you will be a great mother."

"That's what I'm hoping for. I needed one last adventure before putting my wild days behind me." She grinned and I knew she was referencing the careless nights we had spent at the bar outside of Greenville, seeing how many men would buy us drinks.

"I'm determined to have her in my life, Raleigh. She's my baby girl." Julie deserved a happy life.

"We better get going. It's getting dark and the wind is starting to pick up. We don't want to be stuck here if a storm comes."

Soft kisses on my back woke me up. Dull sunlight streamed through the window.

"It's early," I yawned, reaching behind me for his hand so I could pull him close and lull him back to sleep. It was frightening how easily I had allowed myself to fall into this state of mind, this state of being. It was so comfortable being with Kaden that I had almost forgotten why I was here and what he was doing to me.

He slowly pulled me onto my back and rested his torso above mine. His green eyes, although tired, still looked incredibly handsome. He didn't speak to me at first, but ran his fingers through my tangled hair and kissed my forehead.

"I want to get started early," he said, staring into my sleepy eyes.

If he hadn't kept me up last night, I would have been eager to start the day. But, as it was, I could imagine nothing better than falling back to sleep while wrapped in his arms.

"Please?" He must have seen my disapproval at the idea of leaving the bed.

"I'm not sure when they'll be back."

My heart sank. I swung my legs from the mattress, pulling the sheet around my body and away from the bed. The sheet tightened. Kaden held one end. He leaning across the bed and stared up at me.

"If I could keep things the way they are, I would. You know that, right?"

"I know that," I said, giving the sheet a tug and walking to the door. I knew that Kaden would be happy to keep me for an indefinite amount of time, wrapped up in his sheets, away from the rest of the world. But Ray and

Marshall would be back soon and I knew Kaden would not touch me in front of them. He wouldn't look at me the way he was now, he wouldn't talk to me with the same kindness he had shown me for the past twenty four hours.

I walked to the bathroom and brushed my teeth, washed my face, and glanced at my reflection. My skin was a light shade of pink, my eyes were no longer dead behind my lashes. I had to smile, because even though it was temporary, these limited hours with Kaden had brought me back to life. The bite marks on my neck were beginning to fade, and, although they were clearly a mark of dominance, I was slightly sad to see them go.

I didn't know how long Ray and Marshal would stay. Maybe tomorrow they would go to work and leave us again. But maybe Ray had discovered some sense on the drive to Virginia. Maybe he was one his way back to kill me.

Kaden was waiting for me by the door. He took my hand and led me outside.

It wasn't as warm as it had been yesterday, but the sun was still a welcome site. Kaden hurried us along the dirt path. When we reached the lake he untied the small boat. I waited patiently, slightly uneasy about the thought of being in such a small space with Kaden, unable to hide or run. I wanted to trust him, I really did. But, even though I had strong feelings for him, it didn't mean I trusted him.

He helped me into the tiny boat and pushed us away from the dock. He took the oars in his large hands and began to row. I leaned back against the bench and looked up at the hazy sky. Kaden's rowing set a peaceful rhythm and I found myself becoming sleepy again, and had to sit up to keep from dozing off. Kaden suddenly dropped the oars to the floor of the boat.

"What are we doing out here?"

"Waiting," he said slowly.

"For what?"

"If I tell you, it would ruin the surprise."

The boat bobbed up and down for a few minutes and then Kaden pointed. I followed his finger above the trees and saw the graceful wingspan of a heron. The bird soared above our heads before flapping its wings and landing softly on the water a few feet away from our boat. I had seen pictures of Blue Herons, of course, but had never been so close to one. The bird appeared larger than I had imagined it to be. Its long beak was held high, its blue feathers ruffling as it settled itself on the surface of the lake.

Kaden's fingers rested on my arm while I stared at the bird. I was about to tell him how beautiful the bird looked when he held a finger to his lips and reached a hand into his pocket. He removed a few crackers and handed them to me.

I tossed the first piece close to the Heron. It spun around, locking eyes with me for only a second before dipping its head and finding the food. I smiled and tossed another, this one closer to the boat. The Blue Heron paddled its way to the next cracker, snapping it in his sharp beak. Nearer and nearer he treaded as I lured him in. When he was close enough to touch, I held the last of the crackers in my hand. The bird stared at me hesitantly, his neck craning towards my hand as his feet paddled him in the opposite direction. I smiled, not knowing what else to do to encourage him. His beak was centimeters from my hand when he suddenly changed direction, diving under the water. I dropped the remaining piece in surprise.

The bird eventually resurfaced, a long brown snake clutched in its beak. I sat back and gasped in horror as the snake writhed to get free. The heron looked at me one last time before taking off into the air. Kaden started laughing.

"What was that?" I asked, trying not to laugh with him.

"Cottonmouth," he smiled.

I wrinkled my nose. "So swimming is out of the question."

"I wouldn't recommend it." Kaden picked up the oars and turned the boat around, rowing easily back to the shore.

"Thank you for taking me out here," I said when we were nearly to the dock. The shock of the snake was only the only blemish on a perfect morning.

"You're welcome," Kaden replied, looking at me but not quite smiling.

"Do you come out here often?"

"Not really anymore. I have other things to occupy my time now."

I nodded, knowing he meant me and our current situation. My face sank as we reached the dock. Our time alone was almost to an end. Kaden jumped out of the boat first, before pulling me. We took our time walking back to the house, my spirit breaking more and more with each step.

When we reached the house, Kaden locked the door behind us. "You should shower and do whatever you need to do before they get here. It will be easier for me, and for all of us, if they don't see you."

I gave him a weak smile and nodded, walking away from him and up the stairs to the bathroom. I undressed quickly, turned on the water and stepped under the warm flow. I cupped my hands under the stream, bringing the water to my face and splashing it over my skin. My fingers ran through my damp hair and I turned around so the warmth could soothe my back. I jumped and screamed as I opened my eyes to see Kaden standing outside of the open shower curtain. His face was unreadable and hard as stone.

"You need to stop doing that to me," I tried to smile but his expression remained unbreakable.

"They called. They'll be here in an hour."

"Okay." I tried to act calm about it but the uncertainty of it all was hitting me repeatedly like a balled fist.

Kaden stared at me for another moment before speaking. "I want to..." but then he paused and looked at the ceiling.

"I was hoping..."

I didn't understand why he couldn't finish his sentence.

"I'd like to be with you...again, before they get here."

This wasn't a request. It felt more like a business demand.

"All right," I replied, choking back the tears. "I'll be finished in just a few minutes. I can, um, meet you in your room?"

Just saying it out loud, negotiating sex with Kaden, was like torture. It made me feel cheep and used. But Kaden apparently didn't want to wait for me to be finished in the shower. He pulled his shirt from his body, kicked off his shoes, and pulled his pants and boxers down before I could even start to protest. I backed toward the faucet, shaking my head and smiling.

His body looked amazing in the steam. His broad shoulders and chest were smooth next to the white tile. His abdominals clenched when the hot water hit them, but before my eyes could wander further south, he grabbed my hands and pulled me against his hard body. He kissed me playfully, biting my lower lip and pulling lightly on my hair.

His touch was becoming familiar but my skin tingling and ached for his hands to roam my body. My knees grew weak and my head rolled back. I moaned and then moaned louder as his hand caressed the inside of my thigh. His fingers teased me, and as great as it felt, I realized how sore I was and stepped away from his hand before he could go further. He stood up straight and put his hands on my waist.

"Is something wrong?" he asked, his lips barely moving, his hands pulling my waist into his thighs.

"You left me a little sore," I confessed.

"Did I?" He raised one eyebrow.

I put my hands on his chest. "Just be gentle with me," I requested before pushing up to my tip toes and kissing him on the lips. Before I was done, he had lifted me off the ground and pulled my legs around his waist, pinning me against the wall of the shower.

"Gentle? Where's the fun in that?" He smiled and kissed my neck.

"Kaden, please?" I said, running my fingers through his black hair.

He raised his face and grinned at me. "I won't hurt you, I promise."

I smiled back and then allowed him to take me. My arms wrapped tightly around his neck, his strong hands gripping my hips and thighs as he moved against me. My eyes remained open, as Kaden had requested, and I found myself staring at his handsome face. I could see such a longing, such a passion behind his determined expression.

Kaden caught me staring but didn't look upset or surprised. A smile passed between us and he opened his mouth to speak.

"Raleigh, I can't even begin to describe how incredible you feel."

I was about to respond when I felt the first wave of pleasure rush over me. Kaden smiled as I trembled, showing no signs of stopping.

"It's not only that," I saw Kaden say through the steam of the shower. "Just being around you puts me in a world that I never knew existed. Not seeing you for the rest of the day is going to be torture for me."

"Don't talk about it, please," I said as another wave washed over me.

He understood my plea and buried his face in my neck, kissing softly and nipping at my skin. I squeezed him between my legs as my orgasm took over. Through the heat, I could feel him quiver inside of me as he finished. He held me against the wall and my arms wrapped around his shoulders, pulling him close. We stayed that way for a long time, both of us breathing heavily, using the other for support. He set me down gently when his arms started to shake, taking my face in his hands and kissing me. Too soon, he pulled away and smiled at me.

"That should last me through the day, I suppose."

"So glad I could help," I teased him while trying to keep my legs from trembling.

Kaden's fingers lingered on my face, tracing my jaw and chin.

"Hand me the shampoo," he said after a comfortable moment.

I reached behind me and did as he requested. He took the bottle from my hand and poured a small amount into his palm. He rubbed his hands together and then raised them to my hair. I smiled up at him as he started massaging it into my scalp. His fingers sent tingles from my head all the way down my spine and into my feet. I closed my eyes and held onto his hips to keep myself steady.

He gently guided me under the shower head, rinsing my hair and running his fingers down my neck. Soap was next, and Kaden took his time, running the bar over my body. He rubbed me and washed me until he was certain he hadn't missed a spot. The water rinsed me clean and Kaden held me close. I closed my eyes and leaned against his chest, wrapping my arms around his back and feeling the strong muscles beneath my fingers.

I pulled away when I felt the stream of water weaken and eventually trickle to a stop.

"You should get downstairs," he said.

He reached for my towel and wrapped it around me. He kissed me once more before stepping out of the shower and covering himself with his own towel. I walked slowly out of the bathroom and to the top of the stairs, watching Kaden as he made his way to his room.

"Will I see you at all tonight?" I called to him before he disappeared behind his door.

He turned around and smiled. "I'll come see you after they have gone to bed."

I gave him a half smile and looked away before he could. The walk down to the basement seemed to take an eternity but once there, I knew all I had to do was wait for him.

Chapter 14

I had just made it downstairs and into clean clothes when the dust started to fall from the ceiling. Ray was home, and with him came a feeling that something was going to go terribly wrong. The letter I had written was being mailed to an empty P.O. Box somewhere in Delaware. Along with it, were empty demands that Kaden had created to buy him some more time. No one was going to find it, no one was going to ever read it, so how long would it be before Ray realized no one was contacting them to arrange for my safe return? Did I have a week? Two weeks?

I settled myself into bed, hoping to sleep through the rest of the day instead of staring at the ceiling and wondering what was happening upstairs. But I was unsuccessful. The walls of the basement started to close in after a few hours. The ceiling and floor pushed together and soon I was confined to only my mattress, the rest of the world becoming infinitely small compared to the worry within my head.

The dust stopped falling and I had rolled onto my side, staring absentmindedly at the wall, when I felt my mattress shake. I rolled over and sat up, a smile on my face because I knew Kaden had kept his promise and come to see me. But his green eyes were not the ones staring back at me. Marshal was standing above my bed, a guilty smile on his childish face.

He sat down and I moved to the edge of the mattress.

"I won't hurt you," he frowned, clearly upset that I didn't trust him by now.

I nodded, believing him completely. He glanced up the stairs before reaching into the pocket of his sweatshirt.

"I brought you something," he smiled and handed me a chocolate bar.

I smiled back. *Thank you.*

You're welcome.

I grinned at him before opening the candy bar. The chocolate was slightly melted and stained my fingers. I broke a piece off and put it on my tongue. If Kaden's eggs had tasted amazing, Marshal's chocolate was near euphoric. The sweet surprise nearly made me forget my manners and I was almost halfway done with the bar before I looked up and tried to offer a piece to Marshal.

"No," he said, pushing my offering hand back to my lips. "You look like you need it more than I do." He patted his stomach and smiled at me.

I laughed and put another piece in my mouth.

"Raleigh, do you hate it here?"

His question surprised me. I hadn't assumed he would give much thought to how I found this place.

I nodded my head. *Yes.*

"I don't blame you. I don't like it much either."

Why?

"Why?" He gave me questioning look and I nodded my head. "I don't like what we've done. I don't like that my brother and Kaden are keeping you down here, hurting you the way they are. You seem really nice and I don't think you deserve any of this."

Thank you.

I wanted to tell him that he should leave, run away from all this craziness. But he already knew what I was thinking.

"I wish I could run away. But Ray wouldn't allow it. Do you have any brothers or sisters?"

I shook my head.

"Lucky," he smiled at me. "Ray used to be a great older brother. I used to look up to him and he used to teach me things, like how to play catch and how to pick up girls." He blushed.

I grinned and gestured for him to continue.

"I thought it would be fun, leaving my parent's house and living with my big brother and his best friend. Ray got me a job and gave me my own room. It felt good to be free from my dad's rules. But then you came along and I don't have any freedom. Ray won't let me leave while you're still here. He watches me as close as he watches you. I think he's afraid I'll tell someone."

I swallowed and stared at Marshal. Was he really just as scared as I was? Was he being held captive as well?

"I don't know why I'm telling you this. I guess I just don't have anyone else to talk to. But, Raleigh, I don't want anything to happen to you. I don't want anything to happen to me. Ray scares me. I would try to help you, but I'm afraid he'll kill us both."

Don't worry about me, I signed, blinking back tears of compassion I felt for Marshal.

He stared at me blankly, not understanding what I had told him. Slowly, a smile replaced his frown.

"But I think Kaden feels differently than my brother. He doesn't seem to mind that you're still here."

I nodded my head, agreeing with him.

"Kaden's always been able to talk sense into Ray. He never listens to me."

Why?

"A few years ago, when my mom was dying..." Marshal's eyes left mine and he glanced up the stairs.

"Shit," he swore and grabbed the wrapper from my hands, shoving it back inside his pocket. I leaned across the bed and saw Kaden's shoes walking slowly down the stairs. Marshal stood up and took a few steps away from the mattress, waiting for Kaden to reach the bottom stair before saying anything.

"Kaden," he started, acting as if he were surprised to see him. "I was just..."

Kaden wasn't facing me but I could see the muscles of his neck clench in anger. He pointed to the door. Marshal nodded and walked up the stairs, not chancing a second look behind him. Kaden waited until the door had closed before turning around and looking at me.

"What was that about?"

He brought me food.

Kaden snickered and rolled his eyes.

He feels like a prisoner, too. Ray won't let him leave until I'm gone.

"He's not my problem."

He's just a kid. He shouldn't have to be stuck in the middle of this.

"He can leave whenever he wants."

He's scared of his brother. He's not going to...

"Again, it's not my problem, and it certainly isn't yours."

I frowned, turning away from him and crossing my arms. Marshal understood me, at least on some level, and had shown me kindness without expecting or taking anything in return. It was more than I could say for Kaden.

Kaden dropped to his knees and crawled over to me. His strong arms wrapped around my shoulders and guided my head back to the mattress. He started to pull the sheet up to my chin but stopped when he recognized it as his own.

"I was wondering where this went." He smiled at me and I couldn't help but smile back.

"Don't be upset with me, Raleigh. They'll go to work and I'll make it up to you tomorrow."

I sighed and looked into his emerald eyes. They looked remorseful and tired, dark circles starting to form under them. His lips, on the other hand looked almost as good as the chocolate bar I had just finished.

"You want to kiss me right now, don't you?" Kaden's smile widened and my eyes returned from his lips to his eyes.

I shook my head, pointlessly trying to hide my grin.

"Yes, you do," he said, his face moving closer to mine.

"No," I whispered, completely forgetting why I was upset with him.

"And what if I want to kiss you?"

I blinked. "I wouldn't object."

"And what if I don't want to kiss you?"

"I wouldn't cry," I smiled playfully.

Kaden's face became serious. "Just give me time, and I'll make sure you never want to cry again."

He kissed me before I could stop him to ask what that meant. It felt as if he would never pull away, like he would never let me go. I wasn't scared by his possessiveness. I had grown accustomed to it over the past couple of days. I expected it and almost needed it.

I felt him moan against my lips before he pulled away. "What did he give you? Chocolate?"

I nodded, closing my lips, afraid I had some stuck in my teeth.

"You taste amazing." Kaden smiled at me and bent down to kiss me again.

I giggled under his lips and allowed him to kiss me until we were both out of breath. I fell asleep wrapped in his arms that night, my face buried in his chest.

Chapter 15

I woke up the next morning and Kaden was gone. It wasn't surprising, just slightly disappointing. Waking up in his arms, even if it had only happened once, had been the best feeling I could imagine. I dressed slowly and didn't have to wait long for the door to open and for Kaden to come running down the stairs. He picked me up and squeezed me tight. I closed my eyes and hugged him back.

He set me down, eventually, and ran his fingers though my hair.

"What should we do today?"

The question caught me off guard. I could think of a number of things we could do, most involved him letting me leave, but I knew very few were actually plausible. "Can we go outside?"

"It's raining," Kaden frowned and touched my lips with his fingers. I could guess what he wanted to do.

"I don't mind," I pushed the idea.

"All right," Kaden smiled and led me upstairs to the front door. He hadn't been joking. The rain was pouring outside and the sky was dark with low clouds. I stepped onto the stoop and could feel the mist on my face.

"It's one of the sounds I miss the most, you know? The rain. I remember thinking how calming the sound of it was pattering on my window. I could listen to it for hours." I closed my eyes, not wanting to see if he had a response. I stood there for a minute, trying to remember the exact sound the rain had made, but was interrupted by Kaden's strong arms around me. He picked me off the ground and carried me into the driveway like a child in the arms of her father. The cold rain hit my face and arms, running down my skin in tiny rivers. The droplets fell randomly but softly. Kaden started to spin us in a circle. He spun me faster and faster.

We were both laughing as he set me down, my feet barely able to keep my dizzy body steady. I looked up at his wet face, his hair hanging into his wild eyes.

"Thanks," I said softly. "But I think I'm ready to go inside now." Random gusts of wind chilled me.

I started walking for the house. Halfway there, I turned around to see if he had followed.

"It could be like this always, Raleigh," he said to me through the rain. The wind was blowing his damp hair and his perfectly shaped almond eyes sparkled brilliantly.

"Like what?" I called, not knowing if the wind was loud enough to carry my voice away.

"You and me, together."

I stared at him. I could see clearly what he said, I just didn't believe my eyes.

"Raleigh, say something," he pleaded with me.

I shook my head. "Kaden, can we talk about this inside?"

"Tell me, Raleigh. Tell me if you want it to be like this."

"Come inside," I said before turning around and walking back to the house. His words were pure lunacy. Things couldn't stay like they were. They just couldn't.

I opened the door and was nearly inside when Kaden caught up to me and spun me around to face him. "Think about it," he pleaded. "I thought about it all last night and realized what we needed to do."

"And what's that?" He tugged at the bottom of my wet shirt and pulled it over my head.

"We can leave," he said. "Don't you want to leave this place?"

"Of course I want to leave."

"So, let's go." He was working at the button of my jeans when I backed away from him.

"Kaden, you're not making any sense. You know I don't want to stay here. You know that you are keeping me here for a reason."

"That money doesn't matter anymore. It hasn't mattered for a long time." He pulled his soaking shirt off and threw it on the floor.

"Then why am I still here?" The tears had started.

"Isn't it obvious?"

137

"No. No, it's not obvious."

"You're here because I want you with me. You're here because I needed to find a way to make you see that you wanted to be with me as well."

I shook my head and took a few more steps back, raising my hands defensively as he reached for me.

Kaden looked hurt by my gesture but that didn't stop him. "Isn't that what you want? To be with me? You said it yourself, you're scared, you are feeling something that isn't real. But it is real, Raleigh, because I feel it too."

Tears fell freely from my eyes. I had said that. It was true. I didn't understand my feelings for Kaden but I knew there was a strong possibility they were merely situational.

"Last night was torture for me. I didn't realize how much you had affected me until they came home and I couldn't be with you any longer. What I'm feeling isn't just infatuation. It goes beyond that..."

"What we feel for each other," I began slowly, "may be real while we're here. Taking me from this house to another against my will isn't going to..."

"It wouldn't be against your will," Kaden said, taking a few steps toward me.

"You think I would go willingly?"

"Wouldn't you?"

I shook my head and brought my hands to my heart. "Kaden, you need to understand something. Our time here together has saved my life. You have literally brought me back from the dead, given me a reason to hold on, given me hope. I needed you and the allusion of strength you gave me. But look at the circumstances. I had no other choice."

"You don't think you have a choice?" His arms crossed in front of his chest.

"I could have tried to fight you off. But I knew that was a hopeless effort."

"You could have kept your emotions out of it."

I swallowed the lump in my throat. "I tried." Hadn't I tried? I hadn't wanted to fall for Kaden, I knew it was wrong, but that hadn't stopped me.

"Look, I don't want to manipulate this situation. You think you don't have a choice but I say you do. I say you want me just as much as you need me."

"Prove it."

"That's what I'm trying to do," he said, closing the space between us. "Come away with me. I'll show you how great we can be together."

"No, Kaden. How could it work? What would happen when the day came you didn't want me anymore? When I didn't want you? We would be living with this terrible secret. I can't just pretend the past six weeks never happened."

"The day when I don't want you anymore will never come."

"Don't say that! You don't know that!" I screamed at him, pushing his hands away.

"Yes I do." He glared at me, clearly upset that I was challenging him. His naked chest heaved with every breath he took and his muscles looked tense. His square jaw was tight, his high cheekbones cast shadows in the hollows of his face under the lights of the living room.

"Kaden," I said, trying to speak softly. "It would never work."

"You're just scared to give us a chance."

"I'm scared. Period."

"Raleigh," his face softened and he put his hand on my shoulders. I didn't stop him. "Please don't be scared of me. Don't be scared of us."

At that moment, I couldn't think of a valid reason, other than the voice screaming inside my head that I was insane to even consider his offer, not to agree with him. But then I remembered what brought me into this house. "You're forgetting one thing. If I leave with you, Ray gets away with murder. You and Marshal get away with murder. Julie deserves more than that."

His hands ran up and down my arms. "I knew you weren't going to let that go. You can stay here with me, against your will and with a false sense of happiness, hoping that someone finds you and your feelings for me were merely an illusion. Or we can leave and you can learn to live with the small bit of guilt that comes with it."

"It wouldn't be small. It would consume me."

"You don't know that. I will make you so happy, you won't have time to think about her."

"I've accepted the fact that she is dead, Kaden. What I wouldn't be able to live with is the knowledge that Ray is still out there."

"It's a package deal, Blondie. If he is caught, we all go down. If you walk out of here with me, he walks out too."

"Why do you protect him?" I asked. He released my arms and put one hand behind his neck.

"Why does it matter?"

"I want to know. If I understood why, then I might be able to give you an answer."

Kaden's green eyes saw right through my lie. "Bullshit."

"Fine. Tell me because you want to make me happy. Tell me because you trust me and want me to trust you."

Kaden took a deep breath and started pacing in front of the couch. "Fine," he said, sitting down and motioning for me to join him. "I'll tell you but then you need to promise me something."

"Okay," I said, joining him on the couch.

He took my hands and kissed each of them. "Promise me that you'll think about us. Promise me that you'll give the idea of us a chance."

I had already done that. I didn't need to promise it because it was already happening. But I smiled and nodded.

"Ray and I grew up together. I told you we spent summers with his family, but he would also come visit us in Paris. His parents couldn't control him so he was sent to live with us for months at a time. He wasn't really a bad kid, he just had too much energy. But when his mom found out she had cancer, he changed. He suppressed everything he was feeling and stayed by her side for an entire year. He dropped out of school so he could take care of her and he wouldn't speak to anyone but me and Marshal. He blamed his dad because he insisted on smoking inside the house.

"The day of the funeral, I found him in his room. He was sitting on his bed, a bottle of rat poison in one hand, a bottle of prescription pain pills in the other. He told me, with a completely straight face, he intended to kill his father and then himself. It took me hours to talk him out of it. Marshal was so young then; he couldn't have understood what was going on.

"Since then, Ray has been dependant on me. He came with me to Charleston and worked while I went to school. I could tell that he was still suppressing so much. He started drinking heavily and getting into fights. Marshal and I were the only ones who could calm him down so when Marshal finished high school, we talked and decided it was best if we took Ray away from a big city and moved him up here. He was like a brother to me. I couldn't just leave him to fend for himself. He'd either get killed or thrown in prison."

I stared at Kaden. His green eyes looked strained and saddened. His story, while clarifying the bizarre relationship between the three men, didn't make me feel any sympathy for Ray.

"I know that you hate him and I don't blame you. You should hate me, too," Kaden gave me a weak smile. "But I would be done with him if you agreed to leave with me. We could start over again, leave everything behind."

Leave everything behind. That is exactly what I had been doing when Ray hit me with his car. The thought of returning to my life didn't excite me. But the thought of starting a new life with Kaden didn't seem ideal either. Could Kaden and I live a normal life together? It seemed nearly impossible.

"Kaden? Why do you trust me? Wouldn't you worry that if we ran away together, I would leave you the first chance I got? Wouldn't you be worried that I had agreed to leave just so I could escape you?"

"Our first day together, I would be a nervous wreck. But the second day would be slightly better. By the end of the first week, I might be able to sleep at night." He smiled at me and took my hands.

"You wouldn't always be watching over me, making sure I didn't run?"

"No. I'd make that promise to you. If you gave us a chance, I would never force you to stay."

"How do I know you're telling the truth?" I asked, looking at his face to see if he was bluffing.

"You don't. But just think about it," Kaden said, kissing me on the forehead.

"I will," I promised, a little exhausted from all the information I had learned.

He stood up. "I'll make you breakfast. What do you want?"

"Anything is fine," I tried to force a smile.

Kaden nodded and walked into the kitchen. I looked around and took a deep breath. There was too much to think about, too much to take in. I needed a distraction so my head could focus on something else while my heart figured out what to do. I knew if I listened to my head, my heart would be broken, so I picked up the remote and turned on the television. Flipping through the channels, my body froze as a familiar face appeared on the screen. I stood up, staggered to the small television and fell to my knees. My hand went to the screen as my father's face stared back at me.

"Senator Christopher Campbell," the caption at the bottom of the screen read.

Was he looking for me? Making a public plea for help? No. It couldn't be. His face was soft and he was smiling. His grey hair was neatly smoothed and parted. He was wearing his favorite suit, the one I told him made him look more Republican than necessary.

There were no other captions. He appeared to be listening to something and eventually smiled.

"As I am sure my daughter could tell you, supplemental education for those students with special needs is of greater importance now than it ever was. My daughter was lucky I could afford to send her to private schools, but there are so many kids in need who don't have that luxury. The bill the President is trying to push through the Senate would all but eliminate those federal funds that are allocated for disability research. A large percent of the American population would be burdened if it passes."

The screen changed and the news commentator's face appeared. "And your daughter certainly has accomplished quite a lot, hasn't she?"

"She has," my dad smiled and beamed. He looked proud of me. "She's living proof that a physical disability doesn't get in the way of a successful future."

A picture flashed on the screen of my father and me at my graduation. I had a phony smile on my face but my father was clearly thrilled for me.

"Will she be joining your team anytime soon?"

My father sighed and smiled. "She's been offered a job. I just want her to be happy and if that's with me, then I would consider myself lucky. She's a brilliant young woman."

I smiled. He was finally getting something right. The screen went black. Kaden stood over me, staring at the door with a defensive look in his eyes. Slowly, my head turned to follow his gaze. Ray was standing in the doorway, his eyes were on me and his fists were clenched.

Chapter 16

I stared back at Ray. A thick, reddish brown stubble had grown across his jaw and cheeks, his hair stood on end, and with the addition of his oversized rain jacket, he looked like a crazed mountain man. His brown eyes looked furious and his entire body was tense. How much had he seen? Just the sight of Kaden and I together in the living room, half drenched from the rain, half dressed was enough to incriminate us both.

Ray took two lunging steps towards me and Kaden's hand gripped my arm and pulled me to my feet. He shielded me from Ray's punch. My view from his back was limited, but Kaden kept his hands up to ward off Ray's blows. His lips moved a mile a minute.

Marshal stood by the door, his eyes darting between Ray and Kaden, occasionally to me. He looked confused and I wished he would speak, draw some of Ray's anger away from Kaden. Ray's hands flew in every direction, pointing at the television, pointing at the basement, pointing at me still cowering behind Kaden's back. He wouldn't stop and his screams were so erratic, I could barely tell what he was saying.

"A fucking Senator's daughter? You've been hiding this from me the entire time?"

Kaden reached behind his back to touch me and then moved quickly to prevent Ray from grabbing me. Kaden lunged forward and pushed hard against Ray's chest, causing him to stumble backwards and nearly lose his footing.

Ray laughed and stared straight into my eyes. "You've been fucking her too, haven't you?"

I blushed, my entire face was on fire. I looked up at Kaden who stood with his hands down at his sides, ready to be used if necessary.

"To answer your first question, it matters because once they realize she is gone, we'll be in a shit load of trouble if they find out we've taken her."

Ray's hands were thrown up in frustration.

"Don't fuck with me, Kaden. You clearly aren't in this for the money anymore or you would have written a ransom note a long time ago."

Kaden shook his head and I couldn't tell if he was agreeing with or denying Ray's allegations.

"There are three of us involved!" Ray screamed. "I'm not going to prison just because you felt the need to sleep with her! She needs to leave!"

Kaden shook his head again, his arm reaching behind his back for me.

"You are just as guilty as I am! Murder, kidnapping...what the fuck does it matter anymore?"

Suddenly their heads turned to Marshal. He had been standing there so statuesque and still that I had nearly forgotten he was in the room.

"She should just call her father, have money wired to her account. We can leave her somewhere outside of town, somewhere she can walk to safety, and we can drive to Mexico."

Ray's head whipped around to face me. "How much do you think you can get?"

It will depend on why I'm asking, I signed to him.

"You can speak," Kaden said, "They've figured it out."

I took a deep breath and turned away from him. His hand tightened on my arm. "How much he sends will depend on why I'm asking."

Ray's face distorted into a disgusted smirk. "She sounds like a fucking retard," he laughed and looked at Kaden.

I swallowed the anger in my throat and turned to Marshal. He was staring at me like he barely knew me at all, concern and confusion equally apparent in his eyes.

"He wouldn't send any if he thought I was in trouble. He'd only send people to come find me."

"What would you need a large sum of money for?" Marshal's eyes locked with mine. I could tell he was trying to think of a way to get me out of this house. To get us both out.

"I could be helping a friend? If I caught him on a good day, I imagine I could get ten, maybe fifteen thousand."

Marshal nodded and smiled. "That should work. That'll be enough to get us out of the country."

He looked at his brother and my eyes followed his gaze. Ray was saying something to him which I couldn't see. The smile faded from Marshal's face and his hands clenched. At the same time, Kaden's arm wrapped around my shoulders and he pulled me to his side.

"I won't let you do that," Marshal told his brother. "I'll do whatever it takes to stop you."

Ray turned to face Kaden, his eyes roaming over my body. "And you agree with him?"

I looked up at Kaden who nodded slowly.

"Then we're fucked. If she lives, she'll turn us in. We'll be running for the rest of our lives!"

No one spoke for a minute. I looked frantically between the three men, waiting for someone to speak. Kaden's looked like he was thinking. Ray glared at me and Marshal rung his hands awkwardly around his jacket.

"You wouldn't keep silent, would you?" Ray finally asked me.

"You wouldn't believe me if I said yes."

Ray rolled his eyes in agreement and looked at Kaden. "You wouldn't have to do a thing. I could take care of it and you could just go on living your life as if this never happened."

Kaden's arm around me stiffened and his hand came up to my head, forcing my face into his chest. I could feel that he was saying something that he obviously didn't want me to see. The vibrations in his chest were smooth and slow, comforting but their mystery kept me from relaxing. His hand released my head and I turned to see Ray's face redden with anger.

"Fuck you, Kaden. Don't you ever speak of her again!" Ray screamed as he backed towards the door. He turned and was gone in a flash, the rain outside only visible for a second as he slipped through the door.

I looked at Marshal who hadn't moved. He was staring at Kaden as if he had just made the biggest mistake of his life. "You shouldn't have brought her up. You know how..."

But Kaden must have interrupted him because he stopped talking and looked away. He was trying to suppress his anger, that much I could tell. I wanted to run across the room to him, thank him and apologize for not telling him the entire truth. I knew that standing up to Ray hadn't been easy for him. I knew that choosing a life of a fugitive wasn't what Marshal wanted. That life wouldn't be any easier than his life as a prisoner here.

Kaden pulled me towards the stairs before I could say anything to Marshal. I couldn't see any expression on his face.

I glanced back at Marshal when we reached the stairs. "Thank you," I said and instantly felt Kaden's arm pull me up the stairs. I stumbled up the first few, still watching Marshal to see if he would respond. His face grew more and more concerned, the further the distance between us grew.

You're welcome, he signed just before Kaden pulled me up the last stair and out of sight.

Chapter 17

Kaden pushed me into his room and slammed the door. I felt the floor shake. I turned around just in time to see his hands reaching for my face, his lips attacking mine. I was gasping for air as he picked me up and walked me to the bed, his body crushing mine into the mattress. He kissed me again and again as he worked the jeans off my hips. But it was the wrong time for this. Certainly he knew that.

"We should talk..." But his hand on my face interrupted me. He grabbed my chin with forceful fingers, holding my head still and forcing me to look at him. I expected him to say something but he didn't. Instead, his hand covered my mouth as he lowered his head to kiss my neck and my chest. Why was he doing this? What did he want? I hadn't done anything to upset him this time and for all I knew, he was taking his anger with Ray out on me. I struggled against him, trying to take his attention away from what he seemed so determined to pursue. I pushed on his chest, kicked my legs against his, but nothing helped. I couldn't speak, his hand covered my face and he kissed my neck with such anger that it felt like I might choke. My chest started heaving and he looked up, releasing my face only to kiss me again. I couldn't keep up, I couldn't slow him down.

In a panic, I brought my hands to his face and pushed his head away with all my strength. "Kaden, stop!" I screamed as soon as my lips were free. I hadn't been able to push him very far. His body was still pinning me to the bed but his head was raised enough so that I could focus on his face.

His eyes opened and he glared at me but he didn't say a word. There was no soul behind his green eyes, no hint of a person. He looked possessed. With one swift movement, he grabbed both my wrists with his hands and brought them above my head. Five long fingers secured my arms to the headboard, his mouth once again taking possession of mine. I screamed against his lips, flailing my legs as he started to unbutton his pants. My head thrashed back and forth until I was able to break free of his kiss.

"Kaden, don't do this!" I pleaded. Everything we had built, all the trust he wanted me to have was being squeezed from me. Tears poured from my eyes. I sobbed but he didn't seem to care or notice. The more I struggled, the harder he held me and the more he scared me.

I could feel him reaching beneath my panties, pushing aside the fabric and positioning himself so he could force his way inside. I twisted my hips away from him, hoping he would release my hands so I could fight him off. But his grip only became harder and his free hand pushed against my thigh, forcing me back under him.

"Kaden, you're hurting me," I cried, not knowing if my voice was even coherent. But he seemed to understand. He glanced at me only briefly before closing his eyes. His chest heaved as he took a deep breath, removed his hand from my leg, and let go of my wrists. He rolled off me and I instinctively curled away from him, my knees drawn to my chest, my arms protecting my heart and my head.

I cried out loud, not caring if Marshal heard me, not caring if Kaden stared. It was too much. Everything was too much. Kaden's ultimatum, his lack of control, Ray's anger. I couldn't do it anymore and I willed death to come and take me away. Maybe if I cried long enough, the Reaper would hear me and save me from this hell.

I shuddered when I felt Kaden's hand on my side. "Don't touch me!" I screamed and I felt his hand move to my shoulder. He tried to turn me on my back so I could face him but I shook his hand off, rolled from the bed and stood up. I couldn't stand to look at him but I couldn't bring myself to look away. His eyes were filled with tears but his body was defensively positioned, ready to jump and stop me if I tried to run for the door.

"Raleigh, I'm sorry."

"Don't! Don't you dare speak to me!" I was still sobbing and my vision was blurring from my tears. "Everything you said...everything you promised me...how could I ever believe a word you say?"

Kaden sat up and swung his legs over the side of the bed. I shook my head and backed away from him. "Don't come any closer!" I held my hand up, as if that would stop him.

"I know," his eyes pleaded with me. "You have every right to be furious with me. But I stopped, Raleigh."

"I don't care that you stopped!" I hadn't screamed this much since my mother died and I was forced to live with my father. "Look at me, Kaden. This is me terrified of you! This is me feeling something you promised I would never feel again! This is me realizing that I would never, I could never be with you!"

"You don't mean that," he said, his face firm and demanding, seeing right through my lie.

"Like hell I don't. Do not touch me!" Kaden reached for me and I slapped his hand away.

"Don't do this, please. You know how much you mean to me."

"You're sick Kaden!" I shouted in his face, my tears drying as my anger swelled. "I mean nothing to you and this just proved it. All you care about is the control and power you have over me and I hate myself for giving that to you!"

"That's not true." His face softened as he reached for me again. I shook my head and reversed away from him until I felt the wall against my back.

"You're sick," I whispered again, pushing the hair from my eyes.

Kaden didn't respond and took slow steps to close the distance between us. I looked away as he reached for me, blinking away new tears.

"Look at me," he said, turning my face toward his. He spoke slowly. "You mean everything to me."

I glared at him, pushing his hand from my face and turning so I could walk away. His arm flew in front of me, punching the wall as he blocked my way. I knew I was trapped, physically and emotionally. He wouldn't let me go until I had forgiven him. I wouldn't rest, wouldn't sleep, wouldn't function until I had forgiven him. I knew I shouldn't, I knew it was wrong. But I also knew I would give in.

I turned my head, almost afraid to look at him this time. Were those tears in his eyes? Was his lip trembling? I felt something break inside me and I collapsed to the ground. Had everything finally caught up to me? Was my body just giving up?

Kaden caught me in his strong arms and pulled me into his body.

"You promised," I cried into his chest. "You promised I didn't need to be afraid of you. I wanted to trust you. I wanted to believe that this could work..." but I couldn't continue. My sobs were choking me and I had to fight to the, my hands gripping his arms as tight as I could, afraid he would let go and I would fall through the floor, never to be seen again.

I finally allowed myself to rest against him, his arms wrapping around me and my sorrow in a protective vise. My body ached, my chest burned from the crying, my eyes were nearly swollen shut, and my head spun. I could feel Kaden's fingers running through my hair, his lips on the top of my head, his heart beating against my cheek. Could I really mean so much to this man? Could this mess of a human being in his arms be his everything? I was broken and desperate. Why could he possible want that?

We stayed on the floor of his room until I had calmed down. I didn't understand what had happened to me. Kaden had hurt me, upset me, driven me to my breaking point yet I still needed him. I needed him to help me work through my anger, needed him to hold me as I found the strength to forgive him, needed him to be by my side when I wanted to touch him again. My breathing became steady and my head felt light. My heart still beat erratically. He pushed me away from his chest and lifted my face to his. He softly kissed my lips and ran a light finger over my closed lids. Scared and embarrassed, I opened my eyes and looked at him. He was staring at me.

"Everything," he repeated. "You mean everything to me. And I'm sorry I hurt you."

My heart forced my head to nod in understanding while my better sense prevented my lips from speaking. Who knows what I would have said. I could have cursed him, professed my love, kissed him...anything. We stared at each other for a long time, his facial expression never faltering. I believed him. I believed that he considered me to be his everything. But that didn't mean I wasn't scared of what that meant.

"I should go downstairs," I said eventually, though I didn't move. Being away from Kaden might allow me to think straight.

Kaden shook his head, his eyes darting between mine, his brow furrowed with concern. "You're staying with me from now on. I'm not letting you leave my side with Ray threatening you."

"I don't want to know, do I?"

"I think you can guess."

I nodded and Kaden smiled, kissing me again. "I won't let that happen."

I took a few deep breaths and looked out the window. The rain cascaded down the glass, making it impossible to see anything. I wished my eyes could do the same, cry enough so Kaden couldn't see into my head. He seemed to know everything I was thinking. Even in my despair and madness, he could see everything.

His fingers turned my face back. "Come to bed. You should sleep."

I finally smiled. Sleep sounded perfect. Kaden helped me to my feet and walked me to the bed. He pulled the covers back for me and then wrapped me snug once I had climbed in. I turned onto my side and closed my eyes, feeling the mattress shake as Kaden lay down beside me. His arm wrapped around me, his hand finding mine beneath the covers and lacing our fingers together. I was asleep before I could appreciate the feeling.

Chapter 18

I woke up in a dim room. Had it really happened? Had Ray discovered our secret? The pain in my throat and the throbbing behind my eyes told me it had. I took a deep breath and rolled over onto my back. Kaden was quick to notice, sitting up in bed and leaning over me in a protective, concerned sort of way.

"How are you feeling?" he asked.

"I've been better."

He nodded, his lips pulling into a tight line and his jaw clenching.

"I'm so sorry," he said, reaching for my face and stroking the temple by my left eye. He bent down and I closed my eyes. He brushed a perfectly sweet kiss on my left eyelid before placing one more on my lips.

Why did he have to be so beautiful? Would decisions be easier if he was unfortunate looking? I didn't think they would. My feelings for Kaden, although confusing and admittedly self destructive, ran deeper than physical appearances. All the pain he caused me, all the terror I lived with, was nothing compared to the anxiety of not knowing what would happen if I were to find myself without him.

"Kiss me," I said quietly but quickly modified the request. "Kiss me like you would if we were free of this place. Kiss me like you would if you wanted me to believe you would never leave me."

The smile fell from his expression but his eyes remained pleased. One of his large hands came to my face, tucking my hair behind my ear and brushing my cheek.

"In a second I want you to close your eyes," he said. "I want you to pretend you are anywhere but here with me."

"Kaden..." I started to protest but a finger silenced my lips.

"Please? Please do this for me. If you still want me to kiss you when I'm done, then I will be more than happy to do so."

I nodded and closed my eyes, taking a deep breath. I felt his breath on my face, smelled the sweet aroma of cinnamon and relaxed, trying to imagine I was anywhere but in his room. Hands roamed my body, kisses fell randomly on my skin. I pictured myself in my room back in Dover, the pale yellow walls, the white linens and drapes. The sun was on me, streaming through the windows, and perhaps I was in bed with a former lover. But no one had explored me like this man had. No one had taken the time to learn my body like this one. He knew just where to kiss me, just where to touch me. I could feel the kisses on my ribs, his hands on my waist.

I tried again. Who was the blonde actor my girlfriends and I had fallen in love with over the summer? His acting had been less than stellar but his face had made up for it. But his lips hadn't been full like the ones kissing my skin. His eyelashes certainly weren't long enough to tickle my neck as he lightly bit down on my pulse.

No, no actor would do. It would have to be someone I knew. I tried to imagine Professor Vaughn, the incredibly good looking, incredibly brilliant history teacher from school. We had flirted so many times in his office after class - me always stopping by to get his lecture notes, pretending I hadn't caught all of his words that day. Back then I had imagined what it would be like to kiss Professor Vaughn, but never, even in my craziest fantasies, had he ever been this skilled. He just didn't seem like the type of man who knew how to take care of a woman. He would have let me be the dominant one. Kaden would never allow that. My pleasure seemed to now come before his and the way he touched me made me believe it always would, in and out of bed.

"Kaden?" I whispered, my vision still dark behind my lids. "Kiss me."

His lips slowly left my stomach and I felt him position himself above me. I kept my eyes closed, hoping he wouldn't try to speak to me, hoping he would just do as I asked. I felt his warm breath on the corner of my mouth just before he kissed me. He kissed my bottom lip, then my top lip, then finally sealed my lips with his. I felt Kaden's hand in my hair, Kaden's tongue lightly passing over mine. I felt Kaden's heart beating against my chest, the weight of Kaden's body securing me to the bed. I could imagine I was in my room back home; I could imagine I was on the beach in Florida; I could imagine I was in a luxurious hotel with the plush mattresses and expensive linens. But I could not imagine Kaden being anyone else other than Kaden. I was his. Totally and completely.

His kiss lingered long enough for me to shed a single tear of happiness and resolution. But he pulled away suddenly and my eyes flew open. His face turned towards the door and he strained to hear something.

"What is it?"

"Ray's back."

"What are you going to do?" I asked, reaching up and placing my palm against his cheek.

"Talk to him." He seemed to be encouraging himself to do something he was instinctively opposed to.

"I'll stay here," I suggested, not wanting to see what the two men would discuss.

"No." Kaden shook his head, reaching for my hand against his face and kissing my wrist before lowering my arm. "You'll come with me. I won't leave you alone, not with Marshal still around."

"Marshal wouldn't do a thing..."

"Raleigh," he interrupted me. "I wasn't giving you an option."

I glared at him but then saw the distress behind his eyes.

"We'll finish this later," he said, quickly kissing the tip of my nose before pushing away from me and jumping out of bed. He opened a drawer of his dresser and tossed me a shirt, which I pulled on.

Kaden waited for me by the door, smiling. But I had seen his genuine smile and this wasn't it. He was hiding something. Perhaps it was fear, or anxiety. Whatever it was, it wasn't doing anything to calm my nerves. I tried to put on a brave face for him as I took his hand and followed him out of his room and downstairs.

I saw Marshal first. He sat on the couch, staring at the television, his arms and legs tense, his hands gripping one of the pillows on the couch. He looked me up and down, frowned when he saw my face, and then looked back at the TV.

I looked around the living room but Ray wasn't there. Marshal wouldn't look at me again which nearly broke my heart. I felt as if I owed him so much. He was prepared to give up everything for me and I could do nothing in return. Kaden's grip on my hand tightened and my gaze turned from Marshal. Ray was walking from the kitchen, his eyes red, a funny grin on his face. I could tell from his expression and the way he stumbled across the floor that he was drunk. That much wasn't surprising. What did surprise me was what followed him into the living room. She was young, maybe twenty one or twenty two, with long brown hair that hung straight to her waist. Her kind, blue eyes were lined with too much black make-up and her lips were a bright shade of red. She was tall, probably six or seven inches taller than me, but at least thirty pounds overweight, all of which spilled out of her tight jeans and cropped shirt. Her blue eyes sparkled and she smiled at both of us.

"Hey, I'm Carla," she said, extending her hand and taking a few steps in our direction.

I pulled my hand from Kaden's and reached for hers, not out of politeness but out of habit. "I'm Raleigh," I said, confused by the situation.

Carla smiled and I could smell liquor on her breath. Kaden glared at Ray, his brows creased and his jaw clenched. I took a small step away from him so I could see what he would say.

"What the fuck are you doing, Ray?" Kaden didn't seem to mind that I wasn't at his side.

"Having a party," Ray smiled and held up a bottle of liquor. "Want a drink?"

I looked at Kaden. His arms were stiff at his side and he shook his head slowly.

"More for me and Carla, then. My pathetic excuse for a brother doesn't want any either." Ray rolled his eyes and took a swig from his bottle. I stared at him. His nonchalance was intimidating and I didn't know what he would do next. The bottle fell from his lips and he looked at Kaden with an annoyed expression. What had he said?

"Why else would I bring her back here?" Ray reached for Carla and pulled her close to him. His hands roamed over her back and he smacked her hard on her backside. Carla jumped but giggled and nuzzled into his chest.

"Speaking of," Ray looked away from Kaden and at the girl in his arms. "I think we should get upstairs."

Carla giggled again and started leading the way. Kaden allowed her to walk by but grabbed Ray's arm as he passed. I couldn't see what he was saying but Ray smiled.

"No, Kaden. You already fucked it up when you decided to develop feelings for her." His eyes glanced at me and his smile widened. "What did you do to her eye, anyway? I thought you cared for her."

Kaden released Ray's arm and I looked away. I didn't understand what Ray had been talking about. Kaden had done nothing to my eye and I reached for it, hoping to feel something wrong. But I felt nothing out of the ordinary and I dropped my hands, looking around and wondering what to do next. Kaden stared at me with a mixture of regret and hope on his face.

"Are you hungry?"

I shook my head, staring at him and hoping for some clarity. Was Ray letting me go? Was he turning himself in? Why else would he bring a stranger into the house and let her see me?

"Would you eat something if I made it for you?"

"Not tuna," I said quickly.

His head nodded toward the kitchen and I followed him, sitting down at the table and smiling as Marshal plopped down next to me. Marshal still looked concerned and scared.

"Are you okay?" he asked, glancing at Kaden to see if he would object.

"I'm fine."

"I could hear you screaming..." I was shocked he would attempt this conversation with Kaden still in the room.

It was my turn to glace at Kaden. He opened cupboards and reached for something but his head was turned slightly toward us. "I'm fine," I repeated. "Do you know that girl?"

Marshal shook his head. "I don't know why he brought her here. He's acting crazy."

I started to open my mouth to say something but Marshal's head suddenly turned away from me, his eyes on the ceiling. I looked at Kaden. He was staring at the same place. The two men looked at each other and something passed between them which I didn't understand.

"What?" I asked, looking at Kaden. "What happened?"

"Nothing. Don't worry about it." Kaden smiled and brought me a sandwich. Turkey. Much better.

Marshal sat next to me as I ate. He flinched occasionally and at one point started to stand up but Kaden shot him a look that could kill and he slumped back into his seat, a pained look on his face. I tried again to ask what was bothering the two of them but neither would tell me what was wrong and I finished eating, pushing my plate away and crossing my arms in defeat.

Kaden took my plate and his own, rinsed them off and set them in the sink. He turned slowly and looked at Marshal.

"Are you going to be all right?"

I could see Marshal nodding in my periphery.

"Don't do anything. She'll be fine." But he didn't look as if he believed himself. "It will be better if we stay out of it." Was he talking about me? Or was he talking about Carla? Suddenly it made sense and I looked up at the ceiling where Ray's room must be. What was he doing to her up there? I cringed at the thought of him having sex with her, knowing how foul and disgusting he had been that night in the basement.

Marshal pushed himself away from the table, his chair falling over as he stood up and stormed out of the room.

I stood up as well. "Kaden, what is going on?"

"Nothing," he sighed. "You don't need to be afraid of it."

I blinked my eyes, frustrated at his perception. I had wanted to appear curious, not afraid. But afraid is exactly what I was. I could see the reactions of the two men who were in the room with me, but not knowing what was causing them to jump and wince was scaring me more than anything. Confusion and fear surrounded me like a snake, coiling its way up my body and slowly squeezing me to death.

Kaden held out his hand. "Come upstairs. We'll talk."

Talk? Since when had Kaden wanted to talk? It was like pulling teeth the other day trying to convince him to answer seven simple questions. But if he wanted to talk, I was all for it. I smiled and walked around the table, took his hand and followed him eagerly out of the kitchen and through the living room. Marshal was nowhere to be seen and I assumed he had gone to his room. Kaden turned the corner to his bedroom but I stopped once we reached the top of the stairs.

"Can I shower?" I asked, pulling against his hand as he tried to walk away from me.

He turned slowly, a worried look in his eyes. "No," he said, shaking his head. "I really don't think you should..."

"Can I brush my teeth, at least?"

Kaden glanced down the hallway. Slowly he nodded his head and walked me to the bathroom. I shut the door behind me and took a deep breath. I knew he was right outside and waiting impatiently so I grabbed my toothbrush from the counter and squeezed out the last bit of the minty paste onto the bristles. I washed my face next and gasped in shock when I looked at myself in the mirror. I finally understood what everyone had been looking at, what Ray had been referring to. On my left eye, right next to the grey center, was a red blemish about the size of a pencil eraser. I knew what it was the instant I saw it. I had cried so hard a blood vessel had burst. It looked horrible and I had to move away from the mirror to keep from staring at it.

I opened the door and took Kaden's hand, keeping my eyes on the ground and walking behind him. We reached his room and walked inside. I went straight to the bed, curled up with my back to him and closed my eyes. It had been hard to forgive Kaden earlier that day and I knew I shouldn't have done it. But now there was proof that he had hurt me, not physically but emotionally. He had lost my trust, what little he had, and the red stain on my eye was tangible evidence that I was crazy to be in love with him.

Is it true that you can't help who you love? I always assumed that I would have some control over it, have some say about who I gave my heart to, but clearly I didn't. At least I knew that love was never enough. You could love someone with all your heart and still know that it would never work. It shouldn't work with me and Kaden. Everything, all the circumstances were working against us. But I knew I wasn't strong enough to let him go. I was helpless. Helplessly in love with him, in love with someone who had hurt me, in love with someone who would most likely hurt me again. I needed help, but I didn't want it. All I wanted was Kaden.

I felt him turning me onto my back, his fingers lightly gliding over my eyelids as they always did when he wanted me to look at him. But I held them closed, knowing my eye would be a reminder to him of the pain he had inflicted on me. I don't know why I was protecting him from his own guilt, probably because I didn't want to go through the emotions of forgiving him again.

He waited a minute, stroking my temple and eventually kissing my lids. I could feel that he was saying something to me. His lips were moving and his breath was warm on my brow. His lips trailed down my face and found my lips, kissing them gently. He wrapped me tightly in his arms - protective yet gentle, just how I wanted him.

I opened my eyes and tried to smile.

"I am so sorry, Raleigh. You don't know how sorry I am."

I nodded. "Kaden..." I started to speak but stopped myself. He didn't need me to say how I was feeling. He already knew.

"What did you say to Ray earlier today? The thing you didn't want me to see?"

Kaden stared at me and smiled eventually. "If I had wanted you to know, I would have let you see it."

I smiled back. "I know that. But I'm asking now."

"I told him something that I knew would upset him. I told him something that I knew would make him hate me and want to leave."

"But what was it?"

Kaden stared at me. He didn't want to tell me but wanted me to trust him. "I told him that if he took you from me, he would be just like his father when he killed his mother."

"But his father didn't kill..."

"I know that. Marshal knows that. But the way Ray sees it, he killed her. We have gone years without mentioning her because it's easier for Ray not to think about it. The fact that I brought it up at all still shocks me."

I was silent. I didn't know what to say and looked deep into Kaden's eyes. We were still staring at each other when he winced and glanced at the door. I knew it had to be Ray and Carla.

"What is it?"

Kaden shook his head and smiled at me. "From now on, I'm only going to make love to you. Nothing violent, nothing forced."

I smiled, wishing it had always been like that, hating myself for believing it always would be.

"It's true," Kaden assured me. "I want you to know that if you ever want to be with me that way again, I will be making love to you. Every touch should be gentle, every scream should be one of pleasure, every kiss should mean forever."

Did he really just say forever? That seemed like such a long time but an eternity with Kaden would never be enough.

"You need to understand that I am sorry," he continued. "I know I've told you that already, but it doesn't look like you believe me. So, here it is again: I'm so incredibly sorry. About everything. I should have listened to my head instead of being selfish. I should have taken you straight to a hospital, turned myself in and prayed that you would forgive me. But the second I saw you, I didn't see how scared you were, I didn't see how much pain you were in, I just saw something I needed. The life in your eyes was what had me. I made up everything else on a whim, convincing Ray and Marshal we could ransom you, convincing myself you meant nothing to me. You have no idea how scared I was when I found out who your father was. But I just needed more time to see if what I felt was real. I'm crazy, I know that. I'm suicidal for thinking I could ever get away with this. But I'd never fallen for anyone or anything so instantaneously."

I stared up at him, shocked at his confession. He had known from the beginning.

"I've hurt you so badly, Raleigh. I've hurt you because I was afraid you would hurt me in return. Not giving you an option to reject me was the easiest way for me to cope. You were so fragile, so scared. I knew that I could keep you forever if I wanted. Keep you frightened and needing something to hold on to. But I don't want that anymore. I want you to love me for who I am, not for who you've wanted or needed me to be these past weeks."

Love? He'd said the word, not me. "But you don't know me, Kaden. You see me as this scared girl who gives in too easily. You see me as a stuck-up senator's daughter who ran away from the luxuries of home because she was bored. But that's not me. How do you know you'll want the real me? All of me?"

Kaden smiled. "Believe me, Blondie, I see so much more of you than that. I know you better than you realize and I know with absolute certainty that I want you, the real you, any and all parts of you. Sometimes you just know these things."

"Or you just want them badly enough to make it work," I suggested.

"Raleigh..." Kaden took my face in his hands and looked as if he were going to say something. I could see it in his eyes, he knew that I loved him in my own desperate and twisted way, he knew that I wanted to be with him and attempt to create an honest relationship out of whatever it was we had started. My eyes closed as he kissed me. He kissed me again and again, the familiar heat rising in our bodies as our clothes fell to the floor and our senses heightened.

We made love for what seemed like hours that night, neither of us wanting to stop. It wasn't exhausting, it certainly wasn't rushed, we were thrown into the arms of passion and there is where we wanted to stay. I was drowning in him but I wasn't scared and when I closed my eyes that night, his arm wrapped around my shoulder as my head rested on his chest, I knew that he would never leave me.

Chapter 19

Kaden's fingers on my face were the first thing I felt the next morning. I blinked my eyes open and saw him beside me looking incredibly tired and worried. Had something happened last night?

I gave him a sleepy smile and moved closer to him, burying my face in his chest. His arm wrapped around my shoulder. I had very nearly fallen asleep again when I felt him climbing out of bed.

I sat up and rubbed my face to keep myself awake. That's when I noticed my backpack on the floor of his room and one of my t-shirts at the foot of the bed.

"What's going on?" I asked hesitantly, scared of the answer I might receive.

Kaden stood by his closet looking sad. "We're leaving today."

My eyebrows rose as I considered his answer. "Where are we going?"

"The bank." His lips moved quickly.

"All of us?"

"Yes," Kaden answered tersely. His demeanor had suddenly changed. "Please get dressed. It's a long drive and I want to be there when it opens."

I blinked, unsure of what to make of his actions and words but knowing it would be pointless to ask for clarification. I quickly pulled on my jeans and reached for my shirt on the bed. *My* shirt, one of the dozens I hadn't seen in weeks. I lifted the material to my face and inhaled deeply. It was clean and the fabric felt soft against my skin.

As soon as I was ready, Kaden picked up my giant backpack and slung it over his shoulder, opening the door and not waiting for me as he walked down the stairs. Marshal and Ray were at the bottom and I couldn't help but notice the incredibly hostile glance that passed between the eldest brother and Kaden. But Marshal was smiling, a small knapsack in one hand, a bottle of water in the other. He winked at me as I came down the stairs and stood next to him.

No one said a word as the four of us made our way to the car. Kaden carried my bag. Ray and Marshal climbed into the front of the car. I took one last look at the house. The trees waved a final goodbye in the morning breeze, the sun just barely high enough to cast a shadow. Is it strange that the house now appeared different to me? The first time I had seen it, it had appeared quaint – a perfect cabin getaway. Now it looked like a home. Yet walking out the front door for the last time felt like being released from prison. I wouldn't shed any tears upon leaving this place. I wouldn't shed any tears for the days spent in the basement, the days spent in Kaden's bed, the days spent at the lake. I stared at the yellow trim and brick façade as we drove away.

After only a few minutes of driving, the coast appeared. Rain fell from dark clouds offshore but directly above us there was sunlight. Kaden was to my left, his face turned away from me, watching the trees whiz by. His hand rested casually on the seat between us and I glanced at the two men in the front before carefully reaching for him. My fingers wrapped around his and I gave him a quick squeeze before releasing his hand and smiling.

But Kaden barely reacted. He glanced down for only a second while our fingers still touched, his jaw tight. He quickly turned his attention away. I held my breath, waiting to see if he would do anything else. But he didn't. He sat there, still as a stone. Shaking my head, I turned away from him and watched the storm approach the shore.

We eventually came to a small town. We drove down the main street, the buildings on either side worn from the constant lashings of the seaside weather. But as we ventured further into town, the streets seemed to liven up a little. Brightly colored awnings, colorful flower boxes and charming antique street lights brightened the scenery. A branch of a major bank was comfortably nestled at one corner of the town's square.

Ray pulled the car to a stop just outside the bank and I stared at the posters and advertisements in the windows. Not much had changed. I suppose I had expected the world to be a dramatically different place since I last saw it. But the security guard was still carrying his nightstick in his back belt loop, the slogans were still promising the same customer service, and the advertised rates hadn't changed much at all.

I felt the car shake. Kaden closed his door and walked around to open mine. I glanced at Marshal in the front seat. His face craned around the headrest so he could look at me. "Goodbye," I saw him say, unsure if he made a sound or not.

Goodbye, I signed and was rewarded with a small smile. *Thank you.*

I climbed out of the car after Kaden opened my door, and Marshall followed me out. He was trying to hold back tears. Kaden waited for me a few feet away. He didn't reach for me or motion for me to follow him so I turned toward Marshal and smiled.

"Are you going to be okay?" he asked, a few tears rolling down his cheeks.

I shrugged my shoulders but nodded at the same time. "I'll be fine."

"I'm sorry that this didn't happen sooner. I should have..."

But I shook my head. What Marshal had done had been heroic. Standing up to Ray had been the bravest thing I had ever witnessed. But how could I tell him that? How could I tell this boy who had helped kill my friend, who had helped keep me imprisoned in his basement for weeks, that I was grateful for his actions?

Marshal closed his eyes, clearly accepting that he had lost the battle and broke into sobs. It was more than I could stand and I reached forward and wrapped my arms around his shoulders. The boy shook in my arms before he eventually embraced me as well, holding me tight and crying into my neck. It was the closest physical contact we had ever shared. Probably the only physical contact Marshal had experienced with another person for quite some time.

Standing there, just outside the bank, the wind already whipping my hair, I realized Marshal was the one certainty I had. I knew my feelings for Kaden were wrong but I couldn't deny them. They just swam circles around my head and made me dizzy. But I knew Marshal. I knew his character, I knew his struggles. I knew he only wanted the best for me and as I held him close I felt myself start to cry, not from relief but because I knew I would miss him. He had been my hero, my unconditional friend.

"If there was any good in this entire mess, it would be you," I whispered to him. I felt his chest sob against mine and his arms tightened around my waist. But soon he reached for my face and kissed my forehead, never looking me in the eye as he turned away and climbed back into the car. I looked around, blinking back my tears before walking towards the bank, Kaden close by my side.

Already, at this early hour of the morning, people were waiting in line for the teller. I took my place at the end and watched Kaden reach for something in his pocket. He took out my passport and handed it to me, my identification returned without a word being spoken. I looked at the dark blue cover, the gold seal starting to fade. Surreal didn't even begin to describe how I was feeling. I was giddy with excitement, wanting to scream my new found freedom to the world. Yet I was terrified as well, not knowing how Kaden and I would get along in this new world.

We watched Ray's car pull out of sight.

"Where are we going after this?" His green eyes sparkled in a way I had never seen before.

He glanced around nervously. Finally he shook his head. "Anywhere you want," he said with a forced smile.

"I thought you would have had this figured out."

"I do. I mean, I will. We'll figure it out." He glanced outside and then at the clock on the wall.

"Kaden?" His ever confident demeanor had been replaced with a worried and tense one, something I wasn't accustomed to. Was he second guessing his decision? Was he not ready to be with me like he had promised? Had something happened while I was sleeping that made him change his mind?

He answered me with a nod of his head and gestured for me to turn around. The teller was waiting and I walked slowly toward the booth.

"What can I do for you today?" she asked. She wasn't smiling, she wasn't frowning. She looked like a robot, all of her movements and words probably too repetitive for her liking.

"I'd like to close my account," I answered, passing her my identification. "Unfortunately, I've lost my check card."

She sighed but took the document and turned to her computer. I watched her tap away at the keys, not even blinking as she flipped through screen after screen. Her eyebrows rose once, I can only assume in shock at the balance of my account, but her fingers kept moving rapidly above the keyboard. I felt Kaden move behind me, his chest pressing into my back as his hands held me by the hips, pulling me closer to him. I felt his lips on my neck, his tongue lightly tasting my skin.

"Stop," I whispered, smiling and blushing at the gesture. This was more like him. I shrugged him off when he didn't stop and turned to face him. His eyes looked incredibly sad, almost desperate.

"Hey," I said quietly. "It's just you and me now. We'll be all right."

Kaden stared at me. Did he not believe me? Did he not want that anymore? It had only been a day since he had made the promise to want me forever. Certainly he hadn't changed his mind so quickly. Eventually he nodded toward the teller and I turned around, my mood dropping faster than a brick in water.

"Miss Winters, how would you like the balance?"

I answered quickly. "Large bills."

The teller nodded and excused herself, mumbling something about finding a manager to get an approval. I turned back to Kaden who was still staring at me.

"You're scaring me."

He looked hurt and apologetic. "I don't mean to be."

"This is what you want, isn't it? For you and me to be together?"

"It is. You will always be what I want."

"So why are you staring at me like you will never see me again?"

"Do you forgive me?" He ignored my question and countered with his own.

"For what?" For everything? I knew I could never forgive him for everything he had done to me. But I loved him enough to move past it.

"For hurting you."

"Yes. I thought we got over this last night."

"Did we? You never gave me an answer."

"Kaden," I could feel that my voice was rising. "I forgive you..."

"You don't look like it," Kaden interrupted me and his face looked like stone.

"I may not look like it, but I'm telling you that I forgive you. I want to be with you, I want to you to take me away from here and we can disappear together."

"Disappear? Is that really what you want to do?"

"Yes," I gave him a definite answer. "I left home to disappear and I found you. And now, you're all I want."

"There won't be anyone or anything you'll miss once I take you away?"

"No."

"You're lying."

I inhaled. He knew me so well yet I couldn't understand why he was questioning me now. I turned around and crossed my arms, waiting for the teller to return. She walked slowly back to the counter, a stack of bills in her grasp. It amazed me that twenty five thousand dollars fit so easily in her hand, it looked like such a small sum when placed in front of me.

"Would you like a bag for this?"

"Yes, please," I answered meekly. Nothing seemed right about this. I didn't even know if I wanted to do this anymore.

The teller reached somewhere under the counter and pulled out a wide yellow envelope, put the bills inside and sealed it shut. The contents were placed into a plastic bag and pushed toward me.

"Is there anything else I can do for you today?"

"That's it. Thank you." I took the bag and walked away from the teller. I knew Kaden was behind me, but I didn't want to look at him. I didn't want to see what he was thinking, or not thinking. I stepped outside and looked around. People were starting to populate the square and the sidewalk outside the bank, their daily routines just beginning. People. It didn't even seem real that I was surrounded by them again. I had seen three faces for two months, not including my own reflection. I should have been in awe at the sight of strangers. I looked for Ray and Marshal in the parked car.

Kaden's hands turned me around so I faced him. I gripped the bag tight in my fist and I stared up at him. His fingers found my face and traced my jaw and cheek. His touch was so gentle, so loving.

"Do you really forgive me?" He asked, his eyes unreadable.

"Yes," I told him again, trying to sound as soft and convincing as possible.

"Would you forgive me one last time, then?"

"Yes," I answered smiling at him. "I don't even know what you did this time, but yes. I forgive you."

He smiled back and bent his head to kiss me. His lips were soft, his hand wandering to my back and he pulled me closer. My anxiety starting to melt away when suddenly his kiss intensified and he crushed me against him. His lip started to quiver but his arms held me strong.

He pulled away and I opened my eyes. His expression had changed, his eyes were so sad and I couldn't figure out why until I saw the reflection of red and blue flashing lights in the windows of the bank. The lights were everywhere, surrounding us on all sides. For one moment, the people on the sidewalk seemed to have disappeared and it was just me and Kaden, standing alone in each other's arms.

"What did you do?" I looked up at him, my heart racing and my head spinning.

"I had to, Raleigh," he explained slowly. "I had to make things right so you would forgive me."

"Kaden, I forgive you!" I nearly screamed at him.

"No," he disagreed with me. "You might think you do. now, but running away with me would only allow you to keep everything inside, suppress it until it consumed you. I couldn't do that to you. You deserve to be happy again."

"I'm happy when I'm with you."

"Liar," he grinned and kissed me one last time.

"Goodbye, Raleigh." He smiled again, his genuine smile, the one that melted my heart. He released me and placed my bag over my shoulder, stepping away and raising his arms in the air. His eyes stayed locked with mine. I knew there was nothing more I could do as police started to rush toward us. My body felt like stone. Kaden was more malleable. A large officer pulled Kaden's arms behind his back and pushed him forcefully to the ground. His head twisted and we broke eye contact.

I turned to find Marshal. Ray had attempted to drive away but police cruisers blocked the path. Marshall and Ray were screaming from inside the car, their hands raised at gunpoint.

A strong hand pulled me away. I glanced back at Kaden. He was still lying on the ground and he had managed to crane his neck around so that he could look at me.

"I'm sorry," he said again. "You are my everything."

"Kaden?" I screamed. The hand tugged at my arm. I started to struggle against whoever was pulling me.

"Kaden!"

"Go, Raleigh. You'll be all right."

No. I wouldn't be all right. I didn't know if I would ever be all right. What would happen to me if Kaden was gone? Who would protect me? Who would keep me safe? Who would keep me sane? My eyes flooded with tears. We were being torn apart. I might never see him again. With that thought, I could feel it happening - I was falling through the ground. I was falling into the nothingness that dwelled beneath the surface of my existence and I would never be seen again.

I closed my eyes and screamed for him. My arms reached out and my body strained to break free from the person whose arms were wrapped around my waist, forcing me away. It was over. My life as I had come to know it, my life as I had been forced to become accustomed to, was over. Nothing would ever be the way I wanted it. Kaden wouldn't be with me and I would be lost without   him.

Chapter 20

The ride to the police station felt like being driven to purgatory. My mind and body hung in limbo between the sins Kaden had committed and the purification my freedom would bring. Nobody spoke to me, no one looked at me though I felt as if I were being judged. Judged for loving a man who had committed a crime, judged for loving a man who had taken my life from me, judged for loving a man who had deceived his best friends. Did they have a right to judge, these men who had just been following orders? Of course they had a right. Who was I to deny anyone their rights?

So there I sat, perfectly quiet, perfectly shocked, in the back of a police cruiser. I would be lying if I said I hadn't been in one before. My prior offenses were straight forward. I had been caught red handed drinking and smoking pot and vandalizing my father's re-election posters. Back then, I knew I wouldn't find myself in any serious trouble. Sure, the newspapers would report it, my credit cards would be taken away until my father couldn't stand to see me mulling about the house any longer, but my future would in no way be jeopardized. My morals and judgment would remain the same.

But this ride would change everything. This day would, with or without my acceptance, change the entire course of my life. Would the paparazzi discover me and snap photos of my low hanging head as I spoke with the sheriff? I seriously doubted this town had ever seen a celebrity, much less a senator's daughter or a fame hungry photographer. My credit cards had already been taken from me and I felt no great need to reclaim them. But my judgment had changed. My morals, my entire mindset were altered because of what I had done, because of what he had done. I no longer knew right from wrong.

The sheriff was waiting for me at the door of the station when I arrived. He was overweight and out of breath and in need of a trip to the dentist. But he smiled from behind his handlebar mustache and ushered me through the lobby as if I were someone special. I knew I wasn't. Not to him. Not yet anyway.

He led me through a cluster of the desks cluttered with case files and evidence to a small office at the far end of the building. This room had thick glass walls and inexpensive furniture. An ergonomic chair was behind the desk and two arm chairs sat in front of it. A love seat was awkwardly placed in one corner and an old bookshelf stood ominously to the side. I was encouraged by a friendly gesture of his hand to sit opposite him in one of the armchairs. I sat down and waited for his questions to begin.

"Miss Winters, my name is Sherman Michaels and I'm the sheriff of this town." I could tell from the way his lips moved, his accent was thick, his drawl exaggerated.

I nodded my head. "Nice to meet you."

He smiled sympathetically and continued. "I don't want this to take any longer than necessary, but I do need to ask you some questions."

I nodded again.

"First, is there someone who you would like to call? Someone who can come get you?"

I froze. My brain flipped through all my friends and acquaintances like pages in a book and I eventually settled on the one person who would take this news worse than anybody. The one person who this small-town sheriff most likely didn't want to deal with.

"My father."

A phone was pushed in my direction and the sheriff stood up to leave. "I imagine you would like some privacy."

Privacy? Yes. I would love some privacy as I called my father and requested that he came down to North Carolina to retrieve me. I would love some privacy as I was forced to answer the questions I knew were coming. I would love some privacy as I began to cry, realizing that my relationship with my father was so strained that he hadn't realized I had been missing for nearly two months. But that wasn't an option.

"Sheriff, you'll have to speak for him. This phone is useless to me."

Sheriff Michaels suddenly turned red and his face immediately begged my forgiveness. It was now my turn to smile sympathetically at him.

"Of course. I'm sorry."

"It's fine. I'm guessing you don't have to deal with this sort of situation often."

"I had a dog that was deaf."

I blinked.

"Couldn't hear a damn thing. But he could sniff out a thief better than any dog on our team."

I didn't quite know what to say but luckily the sheriff didn't look like he expected an answer. He sat back down and lifted the receiver.

"What number am I dialing?"

I told him my father's cell phone number, the number that only a select few had the privilege of knowing. It was the only number I had memorized.

Sheriff Michaels held the receiver to his ear and then smiled at me. "It's ringing."

I smiled back but only out of courtesy. To be honest, I was terrified of what was about to happen. Would my father even pick up? If he did, what would he say? What would he do? And if he didn't, where would I go? I had twenty five thousand dollars still clutched in my hand and no agenda. I could disappear again.

"Hello?" The sheriff spoke slowly.

"Sir, this is Sheriff Sherman Michaels of the Onslow County Police Department. I have your daughter with me and she asked me to call you."

There was a brief pause and Sheriff Michaels stared at the receiver with a strange look.

"No, sir. She's done nothing wrong."

There was another pause and then he put his hand over the receiver and looked at me. "He wants to know why you are having me call him."

I sighed. "Can you put him on speaker phone, please?"

The sheriff nodded and pressed a button on his phone then lightly returned the receiver to its cradle.

I leaned toward the speaker. "Hi, Christopher. It's me."

I looked up and waited for the sheriff to say something. "He wants to know what you are doing in Onslow County."

I looked around the room and then out one of the large windows. Nothing helped me come up with a good answer. "I was hitchhiking."

We both waited, Sheriff Michaels watching the phone, me watching Sheriff Michaels. "No, sir. She hasn't been arrested for hitchhiking."

"Dad," I started to say before another explanation was offered. "I never meant to...I didn't want to stay." But that sounded like a lie. "I wasn't allowed to leave." That sounded more like the truth. And the truth hurt, a throbbing pain that radiated from my heart and ended in my head. "They took me."

"He wants to know who took you."

Did he want their names? Their physical appearance? A general explanation? "Three men. They hit me with their car and were going to ransom me when they found out who you were."

Sheriff Michaels gave me a curious glance. I shook my head, letting him know I would fill him in on everything later.

"He wants to know if you are okay?"

"I'm fine. I'm safe and I'm...fine." But I wasn't, of course. I wasn't fine because my emotions hadn't fully caught up with my situation. I wasn't safe from the memories of Kaden and his house, the nightmare of Ray.

Sheriff Michaels looked me up and down. He had clearly recognized the lie I told. "He says he's going to come get you."

I nodded, blinking back some tears. "Thank you."

Sheriff Michaels gave my father the address of the police station. He could catch a flight out of Dover and be in North Carolina within a few hours. The thought of seeing my father wasn't at all reassuring. Nothing, aside from Kaden's release would have reassured me at the moment. But I knew that wouldn't happen. I would have months, probably years to think about it and right now I needed to just make it through the day.

Sheriff Michaels ended the call with my father. He sat back in his chair and we stared at each other for a minute. He didn't know what to do with me. I didn't know what to do with him. Begging for my kidnapper's unconditional release seemed like a stretch.

"Your father is a United States Senator?"

I nodded.

"I'll be damned. Those boys caught themselves the wrong fish." My heart sank for Kaden. He didn't say anything for another minute. "Let's start at the beginning," he said and took out a pen from his desk drawer. He flipped open a note pad and dated the top of the page. "How did you find yourself with the three men?"

"I was hitchhiking and they hit me with their car. They thought I was dead and put me in the trunk with my friend..."

"Julie Walters?"

I nodded.

"Shit," the sheriff swore. "So you are the girl who she was traveling with."

I nodded again.

"We found her body weeks ago. Just a few days later, some kids came forward and told us they had given you two a ride. We only got a vague description of you."

I waited for him to give me more information.

"We all kind of assumed you moved on, found another ride."

"No."

"Who was driving the car that night they hit you?"

"I believe it was Ray."

"When did they discover you were still alive?"

"Sometime after they hit us. They put us both in the trunk and when I woke up I guess I made enough noise for them to hear me."

"What did they do with her body?"

I closed my eyes and saw Ray and Marshal throwing her from the cliffs. "They threw her into the ocean."

"Why didn't they do the same to you?"

It didn't look like Sheriff Michaels really wanted or expected me to answer that question. It was more of a contemplative thought, something he probably shouldn't have said out loud.

"They thought they could ransom me," I quickly offered. I knew now that Kaden had wanted me for himself, that the money had meant nothing to him. But telling this man all of the intimate details of my relationship with Kaden didn't seem like it would help either of us. I glanced down at the sheriff's hands. He had no wedding ring. Had this man ever loved a woman? Had he ever been loved in return? Call me critical, but I didn't think him capable of understanding the dynamics of our relationship. He didn't have the desire to understand it, the cruel knowledge that was necessary to fully comprehend it.

"How long have you been with them?"

"Since September 2."

His head shook in disbelief. "Where did they keep you?"

"The basement."

"Did they hurt you?"

He looked like a father asking his child if they were being bullied at school. Did they hurt me? Such a simple question with such a multitude of complicated answers.

"Yes."

"Could you elaborate?"

I sighed. I could elaborate. But I didn't necessarily want to. "They hit me with their car. I'm pretty sure one of my ribs was broken. They kept me locked in the basement without much food. Ray hit me once."

"But none of them tried anything else?"

Suddenly I was shaking all over. "Yes." Sheriff Michaels must have sensed my discomfort.

"Would you prefer to talk to a female officer about this?"

I let out a small sob. "It really doesn't matter."

"Okay." I think he wished I would have agreed to his offer. "You don't have to go into detail. I'm just going to ask you questions and you can answer yes or no."

I nodded, tears falling from my eyes like rain against a window pane.

"Did these men force you to have sexual intercourse with them?"

"Yes."

"All three?" Sheriff Michaels looked disgusted at his own question.

"No," I managed to choke out.

"Just one?"

"Yes."

"Was it Ray?" The sheriff looked as if he had known all along.

"No." My crying only got worse.

"His brother?"

"It wasn't Marshal."

"It was Kaden?" Now he was looking at me as if he didn't believe me. Did he know Kaden personally? Did he know him like I knew him? Maybe they had met at town meetings? Maybe Kaden had been an upstanding citizen of this small town? Maybe everything Sheriff Michaels thought he knew had just come crashing down around him?

"It was Kaden," I confirmed.

"I don't believe it."

"I don't want it to be true."

Sheriff Michaels looked shocked by my reply. He clearly didn't know what to make of it. I didn't know why I had said it.

"We didn't quite know what to make of his call this morning," the sheriff admitted. "I knew he was in some kind of trouble but this…I just can't begin to understand."

"Sheriff? What's going to happen to them?" He gave me what he believed to be a reassuring smile.

"Don't worry. I'll make sure they won't see the outside of the jail until they have their day in court."

I blinked through my tears and the first person I thought of behind bars was Marshal. He must be so scared, so confused. In my mind, he didn't deserve anything that was about to happen to him. I didn't know what they were going to accuse him of. But in my head I could picture him in his jail cell, curled against the wall, tears in his eyes. The image was nearly heartbreaking.

Was it right to separate the three men? Were they not all guilty of the same thing? To some degree, I suppose they were. But Kaden had confessed. Marshal had very nearly saved my life by standing up to his brother. But their characters were not the reason they were all behind bars. It was their actions and, try as I might, I couldn't justify what they had done. Not to myself, at least at the present moment, and certainly not the Onslow County Police Department.

I took a deep breath and accepted my new fate. I would answer Sheriff Michael's questions as honestly and plainly as I could. I would let my father collect me from the police station like he had done numerous times in the past. And I would count the days until I could see Kaden again.

Chapter 21

My father entered the police station like a man with a purpose. His grey hair looked white under the florescent lights and the lines on his face, which usually looked dignified, now looked determined. It took him a moment to recognize me, his eyes passing over the emaciated girl sitting in the waiting room. I stood up, half expecting him to slap me, half expecting him to hug me. It was the latter, of course, and as my father's arms wound around my frail shoulders, I found myself remembering how much I had been comforted by his touch when I was a small girl. The way he would hold my hand when we were in crowded places, the way he would sit me on his knee and tell me stories, he way he would let me cry in his arms if I had fallen and scraped a knee, it all came rushing back to my conscious mind and I accepted his embrace as any loving daughter would.

We held each other for a long moment before he pulled away.

What were you thinking?

I had to smile. He was yelling at me but he didn't want to cause a scene. I doubted anyone in the police station would know sign language so I responded without hesitation.

I wanted to run away.

My father inhaled sharply. *You could have been killed.*

203

I know. I'm sorry.

And then there wasn't anything left to say. Most parents would be relieved to find their child alive after a two month absence. My father felt relief mixed with guilt and a delayed sense of panic. He hadn't known I was in trouble. He hadn't realized my absence wasn't by choice.

"Let's go. We have a lot to talk about."

My father reached for my hand. I felt silly, a twenty six year old woman holding her father's hand, but I supposed it was what he needed – to know that I was still his little girl.

His security team led us through the station and out into the early evening air. I had spent hours answering all of Sheriff Michael's questions. I knew they had been necessary though I couldn't understand what good they were going to do him. Kaden had turned them in. He was clearly ready to confess. I wanted to ask about what the three men had told the police but I didn't think it wise. What were they asking Kaden?

My father's car was parked across the street and he continued to hold my hand until we were safely behind the tinted windows. Our two escorts situated themselves in the front of the limo and compared notes on where they would be taking us next.

"Are we going home?" I looked at my father who glanced at the two armed men in front of us.

"Yes. Tomorrow morning."

I didn't react to his answer. It wouldn't have mattered to me if we had left for Delaware that very second. The fact that I was returning home in the near future seemed unreal.

We rode in silence for a few minutes, my father's hands nervously twisting his scarf. I don't think I had ever seen him nervous. He was always calm and collected or heated and ready for a debate. Certainly never without confidence. I stared at his profile. I could see myself in this man: our shared stubborn nature, our lack of patience for mundane things, our derivative view of the world. But so much of me was my mother: my independent spirit, my ability to love. At the moment, I longed to be more like my father, to be able to pick my path and make my way from point A to point B with determination and without doubt. If I had been like him, I would have told myself to move on, forget Kaden, let my body and mind heal. But I couldn't do that. I could still feel Kaden's touch. I could still say, without doubt, that I loved him.

My father remained perfectly still, apart from twisting his scarf, so when he moved, it startled me. It wasn't a sudden or aggressive gesture. His hand dropped his scarf and reached for the console between us and the front seat. He cringed when I jumped, his eyes filling with tears. He quickly raised the window, shutting us off from the security team, turned slowly toward me, and reached for my hand.

"I'm sorry."

I had heard those words earlier in the day.

"Can you ever forgive me?"

"Dad, you didn't know..."

"But I should have," he said quickly, glancing out at the small town.

I shook my head. I didn't want to hear his apology. It would be easier if I didn't have to forgive him, if I could continue separating myself from him in the hopes of justifying what had happened to me. "I lied, I said I was in Europe..."

But my father interrupted me again. "You didn't email or text. I should have known."

"We've gone longer than this without correspondence," I offered, though I knew it wouldn't help.

"I know. That's what scares me. How long would it have taken me to realize you were missing? How long before I started to worry?"

I didn't know what to say. The answer scared me as well, saddened me.

"You have every right to hate me right now, Raleigh. You have every right to be disappointed. I've been a terrible father."

I stared into his eyes and knew he believed every word. The guilt was visible on his face. I realized then, staring at my father with Kaden fresh in my mind, that I would forgive him. Forgive him for what he had done to my mother, forgive him for what he had tried to make me become. I wasn't him and I certainly wasn't going to follow in his footsteps no matter how much he had paid for my education. But he loved me, his little girl. If I could forgive Kaden, I could forgive my father.

"I haven't been the best daughter."

A slight smile creased my father's lips. "I'm still so proud of you."

"I guess we both have a lot to work on."

My father nodded in agreement, blinking back his tears and pulling me into his arms again. We rode without conversation until we reached the hotel where my father finally released me from his arms, where I made up my mind to forgive the past and improve the future.

Chapter 22

If I closed my eyes, I could still feel his hands on my skin. If I closed my eyes, I could still see his face. If I closed my eyes, I could still pretend he wanted me. But I lived with my eyes open and the reality of what had happened was now starting to fade.

"What did you do yesterday?"

I shifted in my chair and stared at my doctor, my shrink. "I watched a movie with my girlfriends."

"Did you go to the theatre?"

"No. We stayed at home."

"Your home or theirs?"

"Theirs."

My shrink smiled at me. "Good."

I felt like a puppy being praised for shitting outside the house.

"What movie was it?"

"A comedy."

"Was it any good?"

"I enjoyed it."

"Good."

Did she expect me not to enjoy things? I didn't feel obligated to be depressed or morose all the time. People always assumed that I didn't want to talk about what had happened but the truth was I didn't mind talking. I wanted to talk about it. Talking about it made it feel real.

I understood that I had to modify certain parts of my story – specifically the part where I had fallen in love with one of the men who abducted me. I hadn't discussed this with anyone, even my shrink. My dad hated it when I called her that. I hated that I had agreed to go see her. I hated that her stupid questions were actually helping me.

"What else did you do?"

"We started planning our New Year's Eve party."

"So, you'll be attending." I couldn't tell if that was a statement or a question.

"Yes."

"Good."

I would be attending. I was even looking forward to it: shopping for the perfect dress, getting my hair and nails done, drinking Champagne and then closing my eyes at midnight so I could pretend Kaden was kissing me.

"They asked about the kidnapping yesterday," I offered, hoping our conversation would turn to my favorite topic.

"What did they ask?"

"They asked why I had left. I told them that I wanted to run away, to be independent for a while."

"Did they understand your answer?"

"Of course. They're my best friends."

"Good."

My friends had slowly started broaching the subject with me a few weeks after I returned home. They took turns staying with me so my father could go back to work. It was Samantha who had asked the first question. We were eating dinner at our favorite restaurant and she suddenly started crying. When I asked her what was wrong, she said she felt like a horrible friend, not knowing that something terrible had happened and that I needed help. I had expected my father to feel guilty, but my friends' pain had been nearly heartbreaking.

I told her to knock it off, smiling and reaching for her hand across the table. She knew what I was like. She knew that I would disappear for weeks at a time, sending the occasional email or text message, only to resurface as if nothing had happened. She laughed at this and dried her eyes. But then she looked straight at me, her gaze as intense as I had ever seen it.

"Were you scared?"

I had been terrified. I had been nauseous with anxiety. I had been in love, an emotion which now overshadowed all the others.

"Very," was the answer I gave.

She squeezed my hand and smiled. "I'm so glad you're back. And I'm here if you ever want to talk about it."

I had initially assumed that I wouldn't want to talk about it. My time at the house would be preserved in my memory, not on display for the world to see. But I wanted to talk about it. I needed to talk about it. Not to this shrink but with people who knew me and might eventually understand how I felt.

My thoughts snapped back to the present. "Did they ask you anything else?"

"They asked what happened to me while I was there."

"What did you say?"

"I told them that I had been kept in the basement. I told them about how the men wanted to ransom me but became scared when they figured out who my father was."

"Anything else?"

"They asked if they had hurt me. I said yes."

"Did you go into detail?"

"Not very much."

"How did they react?"

"Jamie cried. Samantha said she felt sick to her stomach. Kylie didn't say anything."

"Do you think they regret asking?"

"No." I shook my head. "They want to know."

"Even though it's hard for them to hear it."

"I think it's hard for them to accept the fact that it happened."

"Is that hard for you to accept as well?"

"No. I know it happened. It wasn't my fault and there was nothing I could do to stop it or change it."

"Good."

I suppose denial is common in cases like mine. But I didn't really know. I didn't research it; I didn't go looking for people like me so I could learn from them, heal with them. I wasn't in denial. I felt everything that had happened and was going through all the necessary steps of healing. The first order of business when my father and I had arrived back in Delaware was a trip to the hospital. The doctor announced that my ribs had healed out of place. He broke them again so they could be reset. Do you think that hurt me? Nothing hurt worse than Kaden leaving me.

Next came my friends and family who did everything they could to introduce me back into the real world. But I found it difficult to return to a normal life.

And finally, here I was in therapy where my shrink had danced around the topic of my captivity until I practically forced her to ask me about it. By now I had shared with her almost the entire two months I had spent as a prisoner. But do you think that pained me? There was no pain worse than the pain of living without him.

So there I was, living with hurt, living with pain, living with a memory, a phantom lover who had left me. I wasn't supposed to be missing him. I wasn't supposed to be looking forward to the trial where I might have the chance to see him again. That was supposed to be the final step in my healing process: the trial. They would be convicted and I would gain closure. In theory, and in the minds of my friends, family, and shrink, the conclusion of the trial would signify the end of my sorrow, the end of my struggle. In practice, I had little hope of that happening.

"The trials starts early next year," I said, wanting to see how she would react.

"So soon?"

I nodded.

"Are they being tried together?"

"No. Separately."

"Will you be attending?"

"Yes."

"Why?"

"Because if I don't go, then I won't believe it really happened."

"Are we still speaking about the trial?"

"Absolutely."

Her eyebrow rose. She didn't believe me.

"Will you testify?"

"If I'm called to do so."

"Good."

Chapter 23

I looked around the room. I was surrounded by friends and had a genuine smile on my face. The music must have been blaring because I could feel the base pounding through my heels and the champagne danced in my glass. Everyone was having an incredible time. Everyone was in the holiday spirit and happy to see me enjoying myself.

I stood up from the bar and made my way to the bathroom. Perhaps I should have skipped that last glass. I locked the door and then turned to study myself in the mirror. My grey eyes were sparkling, no longer dull, and my skin had a soft pink blush to it. My hair had its shine back and had grown with my improved diet. I wore it curly. I had gained about five pounds and my father said I needed to gain at least five more. I didn't really feel the need.

A gold dress clung to my body and I couldn't help but wonder if Kaden would have enjoyed seeing me like this. This used to be my element, this used to be what I enjoyed. I still felt comfortable; I was still having a great time, but there was always somewhere else I would rather be. The place wasn't specific; I couldn't point it out on a map, couldn't give you directions on how to find it. The place was with Kaden, circumstances irrelevant, geography not important. I finished my Champagne.

I washed my hands as I came out of the restroom and picked up my empty glass. Slowly and carefully, I made my way back to the dance floor to find my friends. A warm hand on my shoulder stopped me and I turned my head, hoping that a pair of emerald green eyes would be waiting to greet me.

"Hey, you."

I smiled. "Hi, Jackson."

"Where are you running off to?"

"I'm not running, believe me."

He smiled, thinking I was referring to a physical act of movement. "What about a dance, then?"

"Of course."

I set my glass down and allowed him to take my hand. His touch, although familiar and warm, was not exciting or comforting. We had, for the better part of two years, been an item. But that was long ago. We had ended things amicably when I left for graduate school and had remained in touch as best we could. It wasn't long before I heard he was engaged and he was married by the time I finished my Masters degree. I had been happy for him. Jackson had always been the nice one, the one who every girl dreamed of marrying once they finished torturing themselves by dating the wrong guys. He had been too good to me and I had walked all over him. Apparently so had his bride. Their divorce had just been finalized.

"How are you doing?" I asked, looking up at him as he held me in his arms, not too close to feel uncomfortable.

"This is the first New Year's Eve I have spent alone in over six years. I'm doing all right." He smiled down at me reassuringly. "How are you doing?"

I blinked and allowed my eyes to stay closed for longer than necessary. Kaden's face was all I saw. Kaden's hands were all I felt. "I'm doing just fine."

"You look beautiful."

Beautiful. There was that word again. The word only Kaden had used with me, and the word which I only wanted to see him say.

"You're wearing your hair curly," Jackson continued. "I like it."

"Thank you."

"How is your father?"

"He's great. He's getting ready for next year's election."

"And what about the election in three years? Is he getting ready for that one as well?"

Jackson grinned at me. When we were together, we always joked about how strange it would be if I were the President's daughter. I would tell him he wouldn't be allowed to visit me at the White House, I would call Secret Security to have him removed if he ever tried. We would

216

joke about hypothetical situations but also about my lack of desire to have the title of First Daughter.

"You know I can't talk about that."

"I know." Jackson winked at me. "I'm just messing with you."

I smiled at him and he held my gaze, a fond memory passing between us. His eyes shifted and I looked around. People were chanting and I realized the countdown to midnight must have started. Jackson stepped in front of my line of vision just as I was about to thank him for the dance.

"What do you say? A kiss, just like old times?" He was smiling like a fool and I remembered my old feelings for him. No matter how short I was with him, no matter how much anger and frustration I took out on him, he still told me he loved me. I remembered how he could always make me laugh. I remembered how he never made me cry.

"Why not?" I laughed, not expecting the kiss to mean anything.

Jackson smiled and took me in his arms, the grin never leaving his face. I kept my eyes open for as long as I comfortably could, knowing very well what would happen the second I closed them. This was Jackson, my old friend, my ex boyfriend. But as soon my lids had shut, Kaden was there. I could smell the cinnamon. I could taste him. I could feel him; I longed to be lost in him.

Kaden's lips moved with mine, the familiar sensations exploding back. He held me close and I could feel his arms flex to pull me against his chest. I ran my fingers through his dark hair and felt my knees go weak as he lightly bit down on my lower lip. I kissed Kaden for I don't know how long. Certainly we were on display, certainly my friends would see what I was doing. But I didn't care. I missed him so much.

When I finally opened my eyes, it wasn't Jackson's big brown eyes that I saw. It wasn't his boyishly handsome face or his auburn hair. It was Kaden: his fierce green eyes, his strong jaw, his broad shoulders, his angular face and his jet black hair. I took his hand and led him through the party, out into the cold winter night. Kaden took off his jacket and draped it over my shoulders.

"Thank you," I smiled at him.

"You're welcome."

He seemed to know exactly what I was thinking and leaned down to kiss me again. God, how I loved him. I put everything into that kiss, wanting him to know that, even after all these months, I still wanted him, I still wanted him to need me. I wanted him to understand that I had been surviving without him, unwillingly but surviving nonetheless. I wanted him to understand that I had forgiven him. I wanted him to know that I hadn't chosen this life, and if I had a choice, I would decide against it.

Kaden seemed to understand. He kissed me as if we had been apart for years instead of mere months. He held me as if he didn't want to break me. But suddenly our kiss ended and he swung me into his strong arms. I laughed. and he carried me across the lawn and into the pool house.

It was dark inside the small house and Kaden didn't bother turning on the lights. He set me down and we stumbled through the darkness until we found a couch. It was small, far too tiny for us both to fit comfortably, but at the moment, we didn't care. I relaxed onto my back and waited for Kaden to join me. Before long, I felt him above me. His chest was bare and I ran my hands over his skin. He took his time undressing me, exploring my body. His kisses were gentle, his touch was sincere but I could feel his desperation. We both knew that we didn't have much time together.

We made love that night, first on the couch and then again on the floor, everything about our intimacy seeming desperate yet needed. It felt right yet entirely forbidden. I curled up next to him, the clock on the wall reading 3:47 am, and he wrapped his arm around me.

"I've missed you so much," I whispered to him.

I didn't open my eyes to see if he offered a response. I wanted to believe that he felt the same way. I wanted to believe that he had told me he loved me, that he would never leave me again. I fell asleep feeling that my dreams had come true.

But in the morning, Kaden was gone and Jackson had taken his place. I woke up to a loving kiss on my shoulder and when I opened my eyes, the legs of the couch were the first thing I saw. I knew, at that moment, I hadn't made love to Kaden. I knew that I would roll over and Jackson would be the one saying 'good morning.' But it had seemed real. I had needed to be with him and my mind had allowed me to do just that.

Reluctantly, I turned over so I could face him. His auburn hair was a mess and his eyes looked tired. I had to smile.

"Sleep well?"

I nodded, still tired myself. "You?"

A yawn escaped his lips. "That was some kiss last night, wasn't it?"

I laughed out loud at his sarcasm. "This is awkward now, isn't it?" Losing him as a friend wasn't catastrophic. We had grown apart since he had been married and only saw each other at random birthday dinners and the occasional engagement party.

Jackson smiled and shook his head. "No. I think it was something we both needed."

He couldn't possibly know how much I had needed it.

"Probably not the best or most responsible idea we've ever had," he added. "But certainly no harm done."

I smiled at him and kissed him quickly on the lips. "Thank you."

He brushed a stray curl behind my ear and held my face in his hand.

"Come on," he said eventually, his smile still relaxed and genuine. "I'll buy you a cup of coffee."

We spent the rest of the morning sitting in a diner, dressed in our formalwear, laughing as friends.

Chapter 24

I stepped through the doors and looked around the crowded courtroom. I gazed at the floor beneath my stilettos as heads turned toward me. I could picture the other members of the gallery whispering to each other about me. I knew exactly what they were saying. I walked to the second row, my father's hand on my back, Samantha's arm linked with mine. 'What is she doing here?' 'Is she going to testify?' 'Why would she want to see this go down?'

And I had answers to all of these questions, though I doubt anyone would believe them. I would testify, not because I had been called to do so, but because Ray deserved whatever punishment the jury decided to mete out. I wanted to witness this trial so I could learn the truth. But above all, I was here to see him. I didn't know how I would feel; I didn't know what I would do, if I would react at all upon seeing Kaden. But I needed to see his face. I needed to know that he was real.

Justifying this need was another matter entirely. I had argued with myself for hours, scolded myself because I knew it was wrong, worried because I knew there was a strong chance I would just end up hurting worse than I did before. What if he didn't acknowledge me? What would happen to me if Kaden acted like the monster everyone believed him to be? Part of me wished that would be the case. It would knock down all hope that I had built. It would nearly kill me but I would recover. I would admit that I was crazy to fall in love with him, that my attachment to him was merely a defense mechanism. I would learn to live with my shame and in time I would move on.

But what if the opposite happened? What if Kaden turned out to be exactly the person I believed he could be? If that were the case, I wouldn't be able to let him go. The idea of him, the hope of something better, it would surge in my head and my heart and I would risk losing both to a man who I couldn't have. I knew myself too well to deny that I would fight against either of these reactions, the good or the bad. I could learn to live with Kaden, a dark shadow in the back of my mind, or I could wrap myself in the daydream, the one where we were together and happy, where I needed him and he wanted me. The line between right and wrong had been erased the moment Kaden forced me into his bed and, even if I had a choice between the light or dark path, I would never be at peace.

My father's hand directed me down the row of chairs directly behind the prosecution's desk. He had a stiff upper lip and looked at no one but me. During the first stages of this process, my father had encouraged me to press charges. I had declined, and my lawyer had concurred, because the North Carolina state government had already taken care of that. And, of course, it would look incredibly strange if I pressed charges against only one man instead of all three. I hadn't been notified of Kaden and Marshal's trials. They were over in a matter of minutes, both men pleading guilty. For Marshal it was kidnapping and accessory to vehicular manslaughter. Kaden pled guilty to the same charges with the additional count of rape. Neither man had anything to lose by copping a plea, other than Ray's good favor. My father suspected they had struck a deal with the state to lighten their sentences if they testified against Ray. I supposed we would find out soon.

I sat on a long bench inside the courtroom and stared at the ground. I didn't know when or if I was going to see him but that didn't stop my mind from wandering back to our time together. With Kaden I never would have worn such high heels. Barefoot and hardwood floors suited me better than black patent leather stilettos and patterned tiles. I remembered how he had carried me up the stairs so effortlessly, how he had held me in his arms and kissed my temple, how he had pushed the hair from my face after we made love so he could look at me.

I felt Samantha's hand on my arm and my attention returned to the courtroom. As I saw Ray enter the room, I realized I had been smiling. But upon seeing his face, my smile quickly faded and a wave of panic crashed over me.

Had he always looked so terrifying? His round face looked hardened, his eyes defensive and volatile. He towered over the two guards who were escorting him in, his shoulders wide and his posture assertive. His gaze swept the crowd until he found my face, his thin lips stretched across his filthy teeth, his eyes narrowed. I felt his breath on my face, smelled the stale rum, tasted the blood that had spewed from his tongue. I felt his hands on my chest, his legs wrapped around me to keep me in place.

I didn't want to show weakness, didn't want him to see that I was still terrified of him, but I had to look away. I turned toward Samantha who was clutching my hand in support. Our eyes met and I could see she was equally as terrified.

"That's him, isn't it?"

I inhaled sharply. I knew that Samantha was referring to the man who she believed had hurt and raped me. But Ray wasn't that man.

"No," I whispered and her face betrayed her confusion.

"Are you scared?"

I was. "Yes."

"We can leave if you want."

"No," I said quickly then tried to smile. "I need to do this. Please. Please stay here with me."

"Of course," she returned my forced smile and squeezed my hand.

We both stood up as a female judge entered the room. Ray really didn't stand a chance. I could feel eyes on me but I focused on the judge and the interpreter my father had hired to sit next to the clerk. I wouldn't miss a word unless I wanted to. I glanced at the jury, many of whom were trying their best not to get caught staring in my direction. They had been picked well. Not one of the male jurors was below the age of forty and if I had to guess, I would say nearly all of them were fathers. The women were a little more diverse. At least two looked to be under thirty and all of them appeared strong-willed, not scared or apprehensive of the process they were now a part of.

The lawyer's opening statements went much as expected. The prosecution horrified the jury with an incredibly accurate, incredibly descriptive narrative of the night I was taken. They painted a picture of filth and sorrow with Ray as the ringleader - his prior offenses, his known deviant behavior. The motive, as I am sure my father noticed, was not as clearly defined. The prosecutor mentioned ransom money and insinuated a twisted longing for his dead mother.

Ray's lawyer put on an even better show. He promised the jury he would blow away the prosecutor's smoke screen. He reminded them of what his client was on trial for: vehicular manslaughter, murder and kidnapping - the first in no way premeditated, the second a false accusation and the third an act of deception, not on Ray's part but on his so called friend's. And desperation. Desperation? Ray didn't know the meaning of the word. Desperate was being locked in a basement with only a bowl of oatmeal to sustain you. Desperate was being held against your will for an indefinite amount of time. Desperate was falling in love with a man who you knew to be absolutely wrong for you. Desperate was not being able to see or talk to this man because he was in jail for the very thing that brought you two together. Ray didn't know desperate like I did.

And then it happened, the moment I and everyone else in the courtroom had been waiting for. I was called to the stand as the first witness. The victim in cases like this is, I suppose, expected to help the prosecution's case by looking pathetic and hurt, suffering and confused. But for me, I felt as if most of those things were in my past. I was still confused, of course, confused by my feelings for Kaden. but I no longer felt pathetic or hurt. My suffering was almost over.

So I stood up and smoothed the wrinkles from my skirt. Up until this point, I hadn't felt any physical sensations. Now I felt it all: my tweed skirt scratching my thighs, the silk of my blouse smooth on my shoulders and chest, my curly blonde hair tickling the back of neck. The leather binding of the Bible against my palm as I took my oath was soft and warm. The wooden chair felt hard against the back of my legs as I sat down and faced the audience.

Hundreds of eyes were focused on me and I stared back defiantly. I knew what the prosecutor was going to ask me and I knew the answers I was supposed to give. But what had Ray told his lawyer? Those questions were going to be the defining moments of my testimony, my unpracticed responses, my raw answers.

Slowly, the prosecuting attorney, a younger man with an expensive suit and trendy eye glasses, stood and approached me, a casual smile on his face. "Hello, Ms. Winters. How are you today?"

"I'm fine, thank you, Mr. Evans."

"Ms. Winters, I'm going to ask you a few questions and I want you to answer to the best of your ability. Do you understand?"

"Clearly," I answered with a smile. He was trying to show the court that my physical disability wasn't a mental one. I understood the necessity of this, but it still infuriated me. I wish he had been direct.

"Can you please tell me what happened to you on the night of September second?"

I sat up straight in my chair. "We had spent the day at the beach near Southport..."

"Can you please tell the jury who you were with?"

"Julie Walters."

"Please continue."

"Julie and I had spent the day at the beach near Southport and when it started to get dark, I suggested we head back to the road and try to catch a ride into town. We hadn't been waiting too long before a car spun out of control and hit us."

I paused, not remembering what details I had been told to leave out and which to include. I waited for a prompt from the lawyer.

"How much of the accident do you remember?"

"Not much. I remember seeing the car hit Julie first and then slide into me. And then I remember waking up in the trunk."

"Where you had been left for dead?"

I opened my mouth to answer but lawyer Evans quickly turned his head to the judge. I glanced to my right and watched as the judge sustained an objection. Looking at the interpreter, she repeated the word 'speculation' and I nodded a quick thank you.

"We'll come back to that." Evans smiled at me.

"Can you please tell us what happened when you were finally released from the trunk of the car?"

"The door opened and I saw the three men..."

"Are any of those men here today?"

I took a breath. "Yes."

"Could you point them out to me, please?"

Slowly, my eyes wandered from the lawyer to the table where Ray sat. I could tell from his posture that he found this amusing. His legs were spread under the table, his elbows and forearms rested on the surface, his torso leaned toward me. There was a crooked smile on his face. His eyes dared me to acknowledge him.

Confidently, I raised my hand and pointed straight at him. "That man. He was the first one I saw."

Ray's mouth twitched slightly as I held his gaze, but he didn't move. He didn't appear to be breathing. I blinked once and then turned back to Evans.

"Did he say anything to you?"

"Not to me, no."

"But he did speak? What did he say?"

"He told his brother to kill me."

"Are you sure?"

"Yes."

The lawyer paused and glanced at the jury before continuing. "What happened then, Ms. Winters?"

"I was pulled from the car and Ray was convinced to spare my life."

"Who convinced him?"

"His friend, Kaden." My heart started beating faster.

"Kaden Prideaux, the third man in the car with the defendant Raymond Birch and his brother Marshal?"

I nodded. "Yes." It had felt strange to learn Kaden's last name from the newspapers. And, while I knew it on paper, I had never seen it spoken before. Prideaux. It was slightly beautiful.

"What did Mr. Prideaux do to convince Mr. Birch to spare your life?"

"He told Ray that they could ransom me."

"Did any of the men know at that time who your father was? Did they have a particular sum or plan in mind?"

"Kaden found out who my father was a few days later. I offered them all the money in my account, twenty five thousand dollars, but they refused it."

"I see," Evans said slowly, glancing at the jury again. I turned my head and looked at them as well. Their faces were a mixture of disgust and concern. Who they were disgusted in, I couldn't tell.

"Ms. Winters, where did the three men take you after discovering you were still alive?"

This time I saw the defending attorney stand up to voice his objection.

"I'll rephrase," Evans promised. "Where did the three men take you after they decided to ransom you?"

"To their house."

"And you were kept where?"

"In the basement."

"Were you given food and water? Clean clothes?"

"I was given oatmeal every morning and I had running water in the basement. They took most of my things from me but let me keep a pair of jeans. I was given some of their shirts to wear."

"Did you have access to a bathroom?"

"A few times a day, yes."

"How long did they keep you in that basement?"

"About seven weeks."

"Ms. Winters, during those seven weeks, did Mr. Birch ever cause you physical harm?"

"Yes."

"Please, tell us what happened."

I closed my eyes for a quick second, willing myself not to look at Ray. But when I opened them, his face was directly in my line of vision. "The first night I was there, he tried to force himself on me. A few weeks later, he threatened me with a knife and then hit me in the face."

Ray quickly sat back in his chair and crossed his arms. His lawyer whispered something to him with his hand in front of his mouth so I couldn't see. Ray nodded and the smile disappeared from his face, a look of concern slanting his eyes and creasing his brow.

I looked back to Evans who waited patiently for my attention. "Did Ray ever mention Julie Walters?"

"Yes. He asked about her after reading that her body had been found."

"What did he ask?"

"How well I knew her? Who else had seen me with her?"

"How did he react to your answers?"

"He was upset. He said I should be killed."

"Were those his exact words?"

"His exact words were 'we need to get rid of her'."

"How do you know he wasn't talking about letting you go?"

Tears started to form behind my lids. I was actually surprised it had taken this long to cry. It was easy to remember the time I had spent with Kaden. But reliving the time with Ray reminded me of how close to death I had been. "Because he had his brother bring him a knife. He held it to my neck until I bled."

"Did he say anything?"

"Yes. But I don't know what it was. I couldn't see him. I could only see what Kaden was saying."

"What was Kaden saying, then?" The lawyer handed me his handkerchief and I dabbed my eyes.

"He was said there was no need to kill me. They could still get some money."

"And then what happened?"

"They agreed that I should write a letter to whoever could send the most money. They were going to include their demands."

"Was this letter sent?"

"Yes. Ray and Marshal left the next day for Virginia so they could mail it."

"And how long after this letter was mailed did you remain in captivity?"

I had to think about it. So much had happened between the time I had written that letter and the time Kaden had turned himself in. It seemed like weeks, but it was really only a matter of days.

"They were gone for one night and after they returned, I was taken to the bank the very next day where the police found me."

"Why the urgency? They had just mailed their letter of demands."

"I'm guessing it was because Ray discovered who my father was." I glanced at my dad for the first time since taking the stand. He had tears in his eyes but looked proud of me. I gave him a weak smile and he tried his best to return it.

"Was Ray scared of your father?"

The defending team objected. It was sustained.

"Ms. Winters, I only have a few more questions to ask," Evans said, clearly pleased with the reaction he was receiving from the opposing council. He walked slowly to the jury and rested his hand on the railing in front of them. I waited for his question.

"Were you scared of Mr. Birch during those seven weeks he held you captive?"

"Yes."

"What were you afraid of?"

"I was afraid of his temper. I was afraid he was going to hurt me or kill me."

"Why?"

"He killed Julie," I choked out as I remembered how kind she had been. "He didn't seem like he had a problem with it."

"Ms. Winters, the night before you left that house, another woman was killed, was she not?"

This question surprised me. We hadn't rehearsed it at all. "Yes."

"Do you know how Carla Lindstrom was killed?"

"I read that he strangled her."

"Forensics concluded that she was severely beaten before she died."

I held my breath, waiting for him to say more.

"Do you know where the police found her body?"

I shook my head. "No."

"They found her in the basement, lying on an old mattress."

I closed my eyes. My tears became uncontrollable. I could see the basement clearly in my mind, the old furniture, the cinderblock walls and my mattress in the center of the room. It wasn't hard to imagine Carla's body on that mattress. So many times, I had thought that very bed would be my final resting place.

I kept my eyes closed for a long moment, the image of Carla in the basement becoming more and more vivid.

"I have no further questions, Your Honor," Evans addressed the judge. She stared down at me from her seat. Her face remained stern but her eyes looked sympathetic. I must have finally looked like victim Evans wanted me to be.

The defense attorney rose from his seat. Mr. Krieger was an older man, around my father's age. His blonde hair had hints of grey around his temples and his short stature was ineffectively disguised by a black pin striped suite. He didn't smile at me as he approached.

"Ms. Winters, what were you doing the night before you left the house?"

The question seemed simple enough. But I was surprised at how much I struggled to find the answer. "I wasn't doing anything. Sleeping, I guess."

"Who were you with?"

I froze. "I was with Kaden," I answered slowly. My eyes flickered to my father and Samantha who stared at me with worried expressions. Evans looked calm but twirled his pen between his fingers at a nervous pace.

"Were you in his room or were you in the basement?"

"I was in his room."

"So you weren't always kept in the basement?"

"Not always."

"Not the last night you were there, at least?"

"No, sir."

The lawyer let a small smile escape his lips and I followed his gaze to the jury. They were now looking at me with a peculiar sense of wonder.

"Tell me, what were you and Mr. Prideaux doing that last night in his house?"

My jaw clenched. "We were...he was..." But I didn't know how to phrase it. We had been making love, at least that was how it felt at the time. That was how it still felt now. But making love didn't seem like the right thing to say.

"Were you being intimate with Mr. Prideaux?" Krieger saved me from saying it out loud.

"Yes," I whispered.

"Speak up, Ms. Winters. Let the court hear you."

"Yes," I answered, sitting up straight in my chair, avoiding all eyes except the lawyer's.

"So you were distracted?"

"Distracted from what?"

"From what was going on in the house."

I looked at him, trying to figure out what he wanted me to say. "I don't understand the question."

"Were you aware of, or did you have any knowledge of what was going on in the rest of the house that evening?"

"No, sir."

"Is it safe to say that your activities distracted Mr. Prideaux as well?"

I scoffed at the word. Our activities, as he called them, had been beautiful that evening. I didn't believe Kaden had used me as a distraction.

"He seemed distracted at first, but not by me. He jumped at some noises he heard."

"But you don't know what noises?"

"No. He wouldn't tell me. But they started after Ray had taken Carla upstairs to his room."

"But you don't know what actually happened that night between Mr. Birch and Ms. Lindstrom?"

"No."

"Ms. Winters, is it true that you led Mr. Birch to believe you were incapable of speech when you first met?"

I smiled at the way he phrased the question. "When Mr. Birch discovered I was alive and took me to his home against my will, yes, I led him to believe I couldn't speak."

"Why?"

"It seemed easier that way."

"Were you not encouraged to keep up this charade?"

I blinked. "I was encouraged, yes."

"By whom?"

"By Kaden."

"Did he promise you something in return for your silence?"

"He promised that he would keep me safe from Ray. He knew how scared I was of him."

"Were you not scared of the other two men?"

"I was."

"Yet you aligned yourself with Mr. Prideaux because he promised to keep you safe?"

"Yes." I didn't understand where he was going with this. It seemed as if we were talking in circles.

"Did he live up to that promise?"

I swallowed. "Ray didn't kill me, if that's what you mean."

Krieger smiled at my response. "Ms. Winters, you've already admitted to having a sexual relationship with Mr. Prideaux. Can you please tell me when that started?"

"Three days before I was found."

"Was it consensual?"

"No," I answered quickly, having convinced myself that was the answer everyone needed to hear.

"Is it true that Mr. Prideaux knew who your father was before Mr. Birch and his brother?"

"Yes."

"You said earlier that you wrote a letter asking for help and that Mr. Birch and his brother drove to Virginia to mail it. Who did you write that letter to?"

"My father," I said, glancing at Christopher who stared back in confusion. Was he wondering who this woman was, sitting in front of a jury and a judge, talking about things he didn't like to even think about?

"So you must have given someone his address?"

"No."

"No?" Krieger looked around the courtroom pretending to be shocked by my answer. "How did they know where to mail it to then?"

I didn't want to say it out loud. I glared at the lawyer until he spoke again.

"Ms. Winters, I remind you that you are under oath."

"Kaden addressed it to a PO Box in Delaware which he acquired over the Internet."

The lawyer smiled again. "So Kaden was aware your father would never in fact read that letter."

"Yes."

"But Mr. Birch was not?"

"No."

"Did Mr. Prideaux tell you why he falsely addressed the letter?"

I was suddenly aware of how tense I felt. My hands clenched the chair beneath me, my legs were squeezed together so tight that my knees started to ache. "He said he wanted more time with me."

"Is it true that Mr. Prideaux asked you to run away with him?"

"Yes." I started to cry again.

"Is it safe to say that he had developed stronger feelings for you than just a physical desire?"

Mr. Evans stood up to object, his face red with anger. Sustained.

"Did Mr. Prideaux ever voice his affection for you?"

"Yes."

"What did he say to you to make you believe that his interest lay beyond your father's money?"

"He said I was his everything." I could see movement in the crowd as I said this, heads turning to whisper to neighbors, uncomfortable shifting in the seats. A new reality had just settled into the minds of the courtroom.

"Interesting," he said before pausing and looking at some notes on his desk. "Ms. Winters, you also stated that Kaden convinced Mr. Birch and his brother to keep you in the basement."

"Yes."

"Do you know why he did this?"

"He wanted to ransom me."

"Well, I do believe we just established that money wasn't Mr. Prideaux's motivation."

"Perhaps not. But it's the reason Ray didn't kill me."

The lawyer looked at me with feigned disappointment. "Ms. Winters, can you please describe the weather conditions on the night you were taken?"

I paused to think about it. "There was a storm coming in. It was windy."

"Was visibility impaired?"

"No."

"No? It was dark and windy, certainly you couldn't see as well as you could in the daytime."

I shrugged.

"Let's move on," Krieger said and continued without pause. "You were hit by a car and survived when your friend did not. Did you sustain any injuries?"

"Yes. A few of my ribs were broken."

"Anything else?"

"Cuts and bruises mostly."

"Did you hit your head?"

"Yes."

"Were you disoriented or nauseous when you first woke up?"

"Of course."

"And you never spoke or moved on your own until you reached the house?"

"No," I stuttered.

"I see. Tell me, how can you be sure you were one hundred percent coherent?"

"I'm sure I wasn't. I had been hit by a car, after all."

"So you were nauseous, confused and scared for your life? It was dark and windy and, forgive me for asking but it has yet to be stated, you are completely deaf, are you not?"

I glared at him again. "Completely."

The lawyer's lips didn't smile and his eyes seemed to mock me. "The defense rests, Your Honor."

I glared at his back until I realized I hadn't been breathing. I inhaled sharply, the oxygen stinging my lungs and throat. Evan's handkerchief was clutched in my hand and I slowly released my grip, smoothing it out on my lap before looking up at the judge.

"The prosecution will make his rebuttal."

I looked back to Evans who was already approaching the stand. He didn't speak until he was only a foot from where I was seated.

"Ms. Winters, can you understand what I am saying?"

"Yes."

"How long have you been able to read lips?"

"I started learning at the age of six."

"Does my speech look different from say that of Mr. Krieger?"

243

I smiled. "Yes. Your accent is much more western. Mr. Krieger has a pretty thick drawl."

Krieger frowned from his seat and pressed his lips together. Evans nodded in approval and took a few steps back.

"Can you understand what I'm saying now?"

"Yes."

He took a few more steps. "Could you please tell the court your favorite color?"

I smiled at him. "My favorite color is green."

He walked to the other side of the railing which separated the audience from the lawyers. "Could you please tell the court your favorite movie?"

Krieger stood up and objected, clearly making an effort to annunciate his words. "These questions could have easily been rehearsed."

The judge nodded. "Mr. Evans, I believe you have made your point. The court is well aware of Ms. Winter's ability to read lips."

Evans smiled. "No further questions, your honor."

"The witness is excused," she said. I couldn't read her face and I had to remind myself that I wasn't the one on trial. I wasn't the one being judged. It was Ray. The fate of his life rested with this judge and jury, not mine.

I stood up quickly and felt dizzy. Steadying myself on the railing, I took a few slow steps to regain my bearings and then quickly crossed the courtroom floor. I didn't have to look around to know that the entire courtroom was silent. Eyes followed down the courtroom and I sat between Samantha and my father, my head held high yet my thoughts swimming with confusion and doubt. I stared straight ahead and then felt my father's arm wrap around my shoulder and pull me into his side. I turned my head to look at him and his eyes were reassuring.

"I love you, Dad." He smiled and kissed my forehead.

"I love you too, Darling."

Chapter 25

Marshal was called to the stand next. As I saw him being escorted through the courtroom, his hands cuffed behind his back, his face scared and his body nearly shaking, it took nearly all of my remaining energy to stay in my seat. I longed to comfort him, to tell him that I never wished any of this for him, to tell him that his actions had redeemed his misjudgments.

His hands were released from behind his back and he rubbed his wrists before placing his hand on the Bible and swearing his oath. He sat with his head down. He hadn't looked at me or his brother and I wondered if this was the first time the brothers had seen each other since the day of their arrest. Ray clenched his jaw and glared at the courtroom. My heart broke for Marshal.

I watched the interpreter and waited for Evans to begin his questioning. Marshal kept his head down through his entire retelling of the night of September 2nd. He cried when he told the jury that he had been prepared to kill me if Ray had commanded it. How he had thrown Julie's body over the cliff and into the ocean. He smiled once when he told the court about the food he had brought me and about how I had taught him sign language. He started shaking when he was asked about how Ray had hurt me by holding a knife to my neck and hitting me with enough force to knock me off my feet.

At first, Marshal only looked at the lawyers and the judge. He kept his gaze locked until Evan's asked if Ray had ever mentioned killing me. Marshal's gaze quickly wandered the audience until he found me. My eyes filled with tears.

"My brother said on multiple occasions that he wanted to kill her, or that he would kill her if we didn't get the money."

"Do you remember the exact circumstances?"

Marshal sighed, still holding my gaze. "Once was on the drive to Virginia when we were mailing the letter. The second time was when we came back and found out who her father was."

"Do you believe that he was capable of killing her?"

"I didn't want to believe it," Marshal said, his gaze returning to Evans and then flickering to Ray's table. "But he had changed so much. He wasn't the brother I had grown up with. It was like he was a different person all together."

Mr. Evans gave Marshal a minute to regain his composure before proceeding. "Mr. Birch, let's take a minute to talk about Carla Lindstrom."

"All right."

"Now, what happened the night Ray found out about Ms. Winter's father?"

"Well, Ray left and took the car. He was angry at me and Kaden for not agreeing to his plan to kill Raleigh. He came back a few hours later with this girl..."

"Carla Lindstrom?"

"Yes."

Evans gestured for him to continue. I could see new tears falling from his lids.

"Ray brought her home and they started drinking. I didn't know why he had brought her there because he had been telling me that no one could know Raleigh was with us. But then she came downstairs and the two girls met and Ray didn't seem to mind. Kaden was angry but Ray took Carla upstairs anyway."

"Were you able to hear any noises coming from Ray's room?"

"Yes," Marshal answered. His lips quivered.

"Can you please describe them?"

"Things were breaking. Carla was screaming and laughing and yelling at Ray. I couldn't really tell what she was saying."

"Did it sound like she was in trouble?"

"Kind of. Sometimes."

"But you and Mr. Prideaux did nothing to help her?"

"No. She never cried for help."

"When did these noises finally stop?"

"Around twelve thirty, I guess."

"And when did you learn that Ms. Lindstrom was dead?"

"Not until the next day when we were in the police station."

"What did you think had happened to her?"

"I thought she had passed out. She was pretty drunk."

"I see. Mr. Birch, did Ray ever threaten you during the time Ms. Winter's was being held in your basement?"

Marshal looked at Ray but he refused to acknowledge his younger brother. "Yes. The first night, I told him that we should just turn ourselves in but he warned me that if I told anyone, he would kill me and her. At work, he made sure we were always together so I couldn't talk to anyone else about it."

"Did you ever think Ray would actually hurt you or Ms. Winters?"

"Raleigh, yes. But I knew that if I kept my mouth shut, he wouldn't hurt me."

"Thank you, Mr. Birch. I have no further questions."

Mr. Evans returned to his seat and I looked over at Ray's lawyer. Mr. Krieger sat back in his chair and stared at Marshal. Ray still refused to look at the witness stand.

"Mr. Birch," the lawyer finally started. "How did you feel when you learned that Kaden had been hiding the truth about Ms. Winters and her father?"

"I don't know. I guess I wasn't really angry or anything. Just confused."

"Confused why?"

"Well, a couple reasons, really. If her father was a senator, it seemed like we should have been able to get a lot more money for her. But it was also scary because, you know, he's a senator."

I smiled.

"A man of power?" The lawyer prompted.

"Exactly."

"Do you think Kaden was scared of her father's power?"

Evans stood up to object but Ray's lawyer rephrased his question.

"Did Mr. Prideaux ever tell you that her father's connections scared or intimidated him?"

"No."

"Did he tell you how long he had known who her father was?"

"He told us he had known from almost the first day."

"I have no further questions," Krieger said with a smile.

Chapter 26

I barely slept that night. I tossed and turned. I knew I was keeping Samantha awake. Kaden would be called to testify tomorrow and I suddenly started second guessing my desire to see him. What if I didn't get the answers I needed? I wasn't the one asking the questions. The lawyers could twist our experience into practically anything they wanted.

I stared out the window at the sunrise, my eyes heavy, my body reprimanding me for not sleeping. Samantha watched me carefully as I dressed and did my hair, knowing I was worried about something but not ready to talk about it. Would she figure it out? I didn't know if I could keep my feelings to myself once I had seen him.

The crowd inside the courtroom seemed to have grown since yesterday and the looks they gave me were worse than ever. There was really no need for me to be there. I had testified, given my performance and there was nothing left I could do.

I took the same seat as the day before and waited while my father spoke with Mr. Evans. I didn't care to know about their conversation and I sat next to Samantha without saying a word.

Ray didn't look at me as he entered the courtroom this time. But I stared at him. He seemed to have changed overnight. The confidence was gone and he looked at the ground. He still didn't appear remorseful. Not that I would have ever expected him to feel that way.

Everyone stood as the judge entered the courtroom. Her face scanned the audience, resting momentarily on Samantha and me, and then she motioned for everyone to take their seats. Once seated, Evans called his first witness. I watched the interpreter spell Kaden's full name and held my breath until I saw the side door open.

A guard appeared from the dark hallway and a dark head of hair and piercing green eyes following him out.

Kaden.

Kaden's face was just as I remembered it, but his eyes were surrounded by a deep purple shadow and his cheeks looked slightly sunken. Yet he held his head high, his shoulders pulled back, and he walked with a jaunt in his step. Was it an act? I couldn't tell. I could only look at his face, his beautiful and perfect face.

The guard un-cuffed Kaden's hands and he twisted his wrists to regain the lost feeling. He looked at the clerk of the court while he swore his oath. It wasn't until he started to take his seat that I felt Samantha's hand cover mine. I looked down and realized I had been gripping her arm tight enough for it to turn bright red. I glanced at my friend and gave her an apologetic smile which she returned with a skeptical frown.

I'm fine, I signed, not knowing if my voice would even work at this moment.

We can leave, she reminded me.

I shook my head and took her hand, careful not to squeeze too tight. But as I turned my attention back to the witness, I knew my grip must have felt like a vise. Kaden stared right at me. I blinked, just once, mostly out of pure shock, and then felt my body relax. Even though we were surrounded by people, even though we were being judged by hundreds of eyes, and even though we both knew it was wrong, we allowed this short moment to pass between us. I knew he could read my face like a neon billboard sign, and my feelings for him poured from my eyes and flew from my lips as I released a small sigh.

He looked relieved to see me. His eyes appeared gentle, his lips stuck in a crooked smile. I wanted to speak to him more than anything. I didn't care who was watching, who was listening. And, if his gaze hadn't been so calming, I would have had to use every last bit of my willpower to keep myself from climbing over Evans' desk and running into his arms. I smiled back as his lips started to move. I secretly wished he was talking just to me and not the lawyer.

"Yes," he said clearly and I realized I hadn't seen the question.

"And can you confirm that it was Raymond Birch who was driving the car on the night of September second?"

"Yes," he answered again, his eyes still on me.

I looked at the interpreter again. "Can you please tell the court about the conversation that took place after Mr. Birch hit the two victims with the car?"

Finally, Kaden's eyes turned to Evans. "Marshal and I wanted to go straight to the police. Ray had different ideas and we argued for a few minutes. Marshal gave in before I did but we decided to move them farther from town before we dumped them in the ocean."

"Why did you give in?"

"I knew Ray would go to jail, prison maybe, because of his past offenses. Marshal hadn't gotten into any trouble before this. I didn't want him to have a record as well."

"So you were looking out for your two friends?"

"Yes."

"Marshal Birch has testified that once you learned one of the victims was alive, it was you who convinced them to take her back to the house. Is this true?"

"Yes."

"What were you going to do with her once you got her there?"

"Ransom her," Kaden stated clearly.

"Can you please tell the court what Raymond Birch wanted to do once you found that Ms. Winters was alive?"

254

"He wanted to kill her."

"Did he, during Ms. Winter's captivity, ever talk about killing her again?"

"Yes."

"Multiple times?"

"Yes."

I felt my father's hand on my knee. I looked up at him and smiled, reassuring him I was still alive and still his little girl. He was close to tears and his other hand was clenched into a tight fist.

Kaden continued to explain. "He threatened to slit her throat after we learned that her friend had been found. Then again after he figured out who her father was. And one last time the night before I turned us in."

I furrowed my brows at this last statement and tried to remember it. But I couldn't. Marshal hadn't mentioned it during his testimony. When had that happened? I looked at Evans, hoping he would ask for Kaden to elaborate but he had already moved on.

"We'll come back to that. Can you please tell the court what happened the first night Ms. Winter's was in your house?"

Kaden nodded and shifted in his chair. "I was in my room reading and I heard Raleigh scream from the basement. I knew Ray had kept drinking once we got back to the house so I ran downstairs and found him on top of her."

"What was he doing?"

Kaden shook his head and I felt my father's hand searching for mine. I released Samantha from my grip and interlaced my fingers with my father's, my free hand resting lightly on his forearm.

"He had one hand up her shirt and the other down her pants."

My skin started to itch from the memory. I knew that all of these questions were irrelevant to the charges against Ray. Evans was using Kaden more as a character witness to demonstrate that Ray's was capable of murder.

"What did he say when he saw you?"

"He asked if I wanted to have a go at her first. He said she was perfect because he could do whatever he wanted to her and wouldn't have to listen to her bitching when he was done."

I felt my face redden with embarrassment. Kaden refused to look at me and I knew it was probably killing him to say these things out loud. I knew it was also killing him to paint his friend as an uncaring monster with the worst of intentions when he knew that his own actions had been so horrible.

"What happened next?"

"I had to fight to get him off her. Then he said that we were sharing everything, including her."

"Did he ever make another attempt to assault her?"

"He hit her once. The night before it all ended, he held a gun to her head."

I gasped but quickly shut my mouth. All the heads in the courtroom turned toward me. I stared straight at Kaden, willing him to continue.

"Ray said that he was going to kill her because she had ruined his life. He said that she deserved to die and that he was going to enjoy killing her, that he wouldn't regret it."

Ray's massive body stood up from behind his desk, his chair flying backwards and hitting the railing behind him. His face was red and he was screaming, his finger pointed straight at Kaden.

"Fuck you, Kaden! You know that wasn't what..." but his lawyer pulled him down, replacing his chair before the guard could reach him. The two shared a few hushed words which I couldn't see and eventually Ray threw up his arms in defeat. I glanced at the judge who glared at the defense attorney with a warning eye.

Evans continued. "What made him stop?"

"I don't know," Kaden answered quickly. "There was nothing I could have done to physically stop him but he asked me if there was anything I wanted to say to her before he killed her." He hesitated and glanced in my direction. "I said what I thought would make him back off and he did. I told him we would leave the next day."

"What happened next?" But that wasn't the answer I wanted Evans to ask. What had Kaden said to Ray to make him stop that night? And why hadn't he told me about any of this? My head swirled with images of the conversation that had happened while I was sleeping soundly next to Kaden. I thought that night had been so perfect, so ideal. But Ray had tainted it for Kaden.

"I called the police first thing in the morning and told them where we would be taking her. I didn't want them to come to the house because I was afraid Ray would try to kill us all if we were surrounded. So I took her to the bank and let her empty her account to give the police time and to get her away from Ray."

"Did Mr. Birch confess to the murder of Ms. Carla Lindstrom that evening?"

"He did."

"What exactly did he say?"

"I asked about Carla and he said that she wouldn't be waking up anytime soon. He said that shooting someone would be easier than strangling them to death."

"Anything else?"

Kaden glanced at Ray. His head rested in his hands, his eyes closed. "He said he hadn't really meant to kill her, that it just sort of happened."

"I see. Did you hear him moving her body down to the basement?"

But Ray's lawyer stood up to object.

"I'll rephrase," Evan said before the judge could answer. "After Ray left your room that night, did you hear anything happening inside the house?"

"Yes. I heard him dragging something downstairs. He was talking to himself, screaming and laughing."

"Thank you. I have no further questions."

Ray's lawyer stood up and stormed toward the witness stand.

"Mr. Prideaux, can you please describe your relationship with Ms. Winters?"

Kaden blinked and I watched his shoulders sink. He pulled them back up and answered the question.

"Well, I kidnapped her..."

"I didn't ask what you did to her. I asked you to describe your relationship with her."

"It's complicated," Kaden said through clenched teeth.

"Complicated, how?"

Kaden blinked a couple of times, searching for the right words. "Complicated by the fact that what I did to her and what I wanted from her didn't add up."

"You are currently serving a four year sentence for rape and kidnapping, are you not?"

"Yes."

Four years? My heart sank. I thought about everything that would happen in four years. I would be thirty years old, my father could be President, my body and mind would have changed so much by then.

"That clearly establishes what you did to Ms. Winters, now will you please tell the court what you wanted from her?"

Kaden glanced at me and smiled. "I wanted her to love me."

"Why?"

"Because I loved her. Because I wanted to be with her."

My face and body froze. I imprinted into my mind the exact way Kaden's lips moved as he spoke those words. My father stirred uncomfortably by my side. Samantha gave me a desperate look, but there was nothing I could do for either of them. I knew that they didn't want to know my true feelings.

"But you were already with her, Mr. Prideaux, were you not?"

"I wanted her to want to be with me," Kaden clarified.

"Mr. Birch and Ms. Winters have stated that you withheld information from Raymond and Marshal regarding the truth about Ms. Winters' father and her ability to speak. Can you please tell the court why you did this?"

"I thought it would buy me more time with her."

"Did you ever intend on ransoming her?"

"At the very beginning, yes."

"At the very beginning," Mr. Krieger repeated and nodded his head. "Mr. Prideaux, when did you learn that Ms. Winters' could speak?"

Kaden smiled. "I had that figured out pretty quickly. She always looked as if she wanted to tell me off."

"And when did you confront her about it?"

"The day we brought her home," Kaden said, looking from the lawyer to me. His gaze held mine in a way that made the hairs on my arms rise. "Ray and I went through her things, searching every pocket in her bag, looking for anything that could help us. Marshal brought her inside and I took her upstairs to get her cleaned up. I told her to cut the act and she eventually gave in."

I frowned at this. The first part of his answer had been so insignificant. Every pocket of my bag, anything that could help them? Why would he bring that up? And, was it my imagination, or had he been emphasizing them to me? Maybe I just wanted to find a deeper meaning, just wanted to find something to hold on to.

Mr. Krieger's next question got my full attention.

"So once you had confirmation of Ms. Winters' ability to speak, why did you keep it from Ray and Marshal?"

"Because it put me in control."

"Control to do what?"

"Control to call the shots. Control to keep Raleigh safe."

"Safe? Surely she wasn't kept safe if you raped her."

My father squeezed my hand and I glanced up at him. He stared down at me with a frightened and helpless expression. I smiled and squeezed back. I was still here, still in one piece.

"Don't you think she would have been safer if you had accepted the ransom money and turned her over to her father?"

Kaden blinked. "I suppose."

"Let me just clarify, Mr. Prideaux. You led Ray and Marshal Birch to believe that you would ransom Ms. Winters, something which you admit would have been in her better interests, yet you hid information from them to buy you more time with her."

It was clever what the lawyer was doing. Clever, but inevitably pointless because Marshal had already testified against his brother. Krieger wanted to show the jury that Kaden had been keeping me, not for ransom money as he promised Ray and Marshal, but for his own selfish purposes. Ray had therefore been misled, tricked into doing things he wouldn't have done under normal circumstances. It was a tough theory to prove but probably the only way the jury would give Ray any sympathy.

"Yes," Kaden answered, looking guilty for the first time.

"So you admit to withholding information from Mr. Birch and his brother with the intent of prolonging Ms. Winters stay?"

"Yes, but Ray would have killed her if he found out who her father was."

"How do you know that?" Mr. Krieger demanded. "Raymond Birch drove hundreds of miles to mail a ransom note which he believed would be answered. His actions tell us that he did indeed want to ransom her."

"He also held a gun to her head and a knife to her throat," Kaden said, his face reddening with anger, his jaw clenching. "He told me that he was going to kill her because she had ruined his life. He killed that girl because he knew I wouldn't let him kill Raleigh."

But the judge held up a warning hand, letting Kaden know that he was out of line.

"I would ask the court for Mr. Prideaux's statements to be struck from the record. They are merely speculations." Mr. Krieger turned toward the judge.

"They weren't speculations!" Kaden screamed, standing up and then immediately sitting down and hanging his head.

"So stricken," the judge ruled.

"I have no further questions."

Evans was out of his seat before Mr. Krieger had finished speaking, ready for his rebuttal.

"Mr. Prideaux, when you first found Ms. Winters alive in the trunk of your car, is it true that you convinced Raymond Birch to ransom her as an alternative to death?"

"Yes."

"And, please tell the court, between the three of you, who vocalized his desire to kill Ms. Winters?"

"It was Ray."

"Prosecution rests."

Kaden's head snapped to the judge and she excused him. Immediately he was out of his seat and quickly handcuffed by the guards. I felt my throat start to close, a sob resting just above my chest. I didn't want him to leave. If I could just look at him for another hour, another five minutes, things would get better. My legs twitched and I fought an urge to run. I clamped my hands into tight fists and pressed my mouth into a firm line so no words could escape.

I watched in horror as the guards escorted Kaden from the courtroom, waiting for him to turn around and acknowledge me one last time. He was nearly to the door before it happened. He glanced over his shoulder, his face calm, his walk steady. His green eyes caught mine only for the briefest of seconds and I saw him smile. I could tell the smile was meant for no one but me and I buried my face into my father's chest and broke into tears.

Chapter 26

I walked back to the hotel room alone that afternoon. The winter wind burned my face and hands but I barely noticed. I was still in love with Kaden and almost entirely sure that he still loved me back. But was someone like Kaden capable of love in the best sense of the word? Love was supposed to be personalized, it was supposed to mean something different to each person. But I didn't know what it meant to Kaden. I didn't understand his definition of love and it certainly didn't seem compatible with the commonly accepted description of the word. But what I didn't understand no longer scared me. I should have been ashamed, I should have been sick with disgust that I relished the love of a man who had kidnapped and raped me. But I was a sick, masochistic girl who went to bed every night praying I would wake up in his arms.

The hotel where my father, Samantha, and I had stayed was old and rather quaint, probably one of the only hotels in the area that wasn't near the highway and that didn't advertise specials for free HBO. The high ceiling in the lobby was painted in a maritime theme and accented with gold leaf.

I nodded at the concierge, made my way to the spiral staircase and slowly climbed the stairs. The walls of the hotel were lined with old pictures and drawings of ships and other sea vessels, all with two dates: their maiden voyage and either their disappearance or the day they sank. The name of the captain was printed below. I wondered if anyone else was staying in this hotel and, if they were, did they find these pictures as depressing as I did? I would have much rather seen ships that were still strong and alive out on the ocean. Why immortalize something so upsetting? Surely, drowning would be a painful death, especially for the captain, who lost his ship and his life at the same time.

But then again, there was something heroic and almost romantic about dying at sea. You fight to save the ship you love and have worked with for so many years, only to have a force stronger than either man or vessel finally consume you and your beloved. It wouldn't be that bad, I supposed.

***

I didn't have to put up with the pictures for much longer. The trial ended two days later. After Kaden's testimony, Sheriff Michaels was called to the stand along with the doctor who had seen me the day I was found. The sheriff discussed Ray's prior offenses, his reputation within the community. The negative review wasn't surprising.

The doctor testified that I had broken ribs that had healed out of place, a result of an injury that most likely occurred five to eight weeks before my visit.

Ray surprised everyone, including his lawyer I believe, by refusing to testify in his own defense. Maybe he knew it was a lost cause, maybe he had just given up, but I could tell after Kaden's day on the stand that something inside of Ray had broken. He no longer held his head with confidence, feigned or otherwise. He no longer searched for my gaze in the audience, hoping to intimidate me with his smile. He no longer showed his frustration or excitement. He just sat in his chair, gazing out the window or scanning the faces of the jury.

The only thing left for Krieger to do was call a character witness, an old and assertive criminal psychologist who said he believed Ray suffered from some form of Post Traumatic Stress Disorder, a result of his mother's ddeath. Evans had a handful of cards to play but chose the one that would hurt the most. He asked the psychologist if everyone suffering from Post Traumatic Stress has a criminal record, if they all kidnap and kill people. The psychologist's negative answer sealed Ray's fate.

I knew what the verdict would be before it was read. The members of the jury tried their best to keep a straight face, but many of them glared at Ray, others glanced at me with a hopeful glint in their eyes. I believe they thought this verdict would change my life, bring some closure to my painful journey. It did, in some ways. But I had known all along what Ray had done. He was guilty of murder, kidnapping, and assault. I didn't needed a judge and jury to decide that for me.

We flew home the night the trial ended. My father needed to get back to work and I wanted nothing more than to search through my old backpack. I still had it. I hadn't removed a thing. All of the contents of the bag were in the exact same place they were the day I was found. I don't know what inspired me not to throw it away. I don't know why I hadn't searched through it in a desperate attempt to remember him. But it was like a time capsule, the things inside preserved those weeks spent with Kaden. Disturbing them would be criminal. But now it had to be done.

I wanted to believe that Kaden had given me a sign that day in the courtroom. *Every pocket of my bag. Anything that could help us.* Those were his words. I knew his eyes had been telling me to pay attention and begging me to do something.

The drive from the airport was torture. I was so close, so convinced that I was going to find something that would change my life. I had thought about hundreds of things I could find in that bag.

Maybe a letter from Kaden, a note that would explain everything? Maybe it would be his favorite shirt, the one he had agreed to let me borrow as long as it smelled like me when I returned it? It could be something to remember him by. Would I take that as a sign that he wanted me to let go, a signal for me to move on?

Samantha dropped me off at my house and told me to text her if I needed anything. I gave her a hug and promised to see her the next day. I walked slowly up my front steps, knowing she would watch me until I had disappeared behind the closed door. The second I was safe inside, I sprinted to my bedroom and dropped to my knees at the foot of my bed. I reached beneath the frame and pulled the bag into my lap. Clothes flew everywhere, followed by old makeup and a few protein bars. Once the contents of the main compartment were out, I dug my hand deep into the inside pocket, the one where my passport and most of my cash had been.

I gasped as my fingers touched an unfamiliar object. I knew it was a key and I also knew it wasn't mine. It hadn't been there before. I wasn't sure if I wanted to know which door it would open. So I left it there for the moment and kept searching. Paper crumpled at the bottom of the pocket, the edges stiff.

I paused, my hand buried deep in the bag. Kaden had been telling me something. He knew I would go home and search for whatever it was he had left in my bag. But I was finally starting to live my life again. My friends no longer looked at me with sad expressions. The color had returned to my skin. My father and I were speaking, we were even affectionate at times. I had Jackson in my life, a man who was now my friend but who I knew could be so much more if we ever wanted to take that step. I knew I would always live with Kaden's memory, but I no longer knew if I wanted to live *in* that memory. Pulling out this key and reading whatever was written on that paper would throw me right back into his world. I would start pining for him again, start remembering all the good things about him, not all the terrible things he had done.

I closed my eyes and tried to listen to my heart or my head, whichever one that would give me an answer. But like the world I lived in, my conscience was silent. I didn't think I had the courage to just throw my bag beneath my bed and pretend like nothing had happened. I would have to burn the contents so there would be no way of knowing what Kaden had wanted me to find. A single tear rolled down my face.

This bag had been my life until I had met Kaden. It had taken me from Delaware to the North Carolina shore. Burning it would be like burning a part of my life – the wrong part, for I never regretted the events leading up to Kaden. My choice to leave home had been made from my

271

own free will. If I pulled this key from its hiding spot, would I be strong enough to make the right decision? Kaden still influenced almost everything I did; he was on my mind constantly yet I had learned to control him, push him to a corner where I could merely observe and feel his presence.

My fingers traveled back to the key, pressing it into my palm and then crinkling the paper as I pulled it from the pocket. Tears now fell freely from my eyes. I didn't want to do this. I didn't want to feel him anymore, didn't want to return to that life where he held so much control, but I knew I would give in. Just as I had so many times before, I would forgive him this one last torture and continue loving him as long he would let me. I clenched the key and paper in my fist, my tears temporarily blinding me as I sobbed on the floor of my room. I knew Kaden would want me to be strong. He wasn't here to comfort me or force me to do anything, but the knowledge that he wanted me to find this was enough for me to open my eyes.

My fingers straightened the paper, which I set carefully on the floor. I took a deep breath before wiping away my tears and looking at the paper.

Raleigh,

I'm writing this, knowing what I'm about to do will hurt you probably more than anything I've done before. I hate myself for hurting you, honestly I do. But I want you to understand why I'm doing this. I want you to be free of me, Raleigh. I want you to have your life back because it was unfair of me to take that from you. It was unfair of me to ask you to run away with me and it was unfair for me to turn myself in once I realized what you wanted.

Do you remember when you told me that the feelings between us were merely circumstantial, that you had no other choice? I told you not to be scared of us and asked you to give us a chance. I'm still hoping for that chance and, as you can see by now, I've changed my mind about atoning for my actions. It's hard to turn yourself in for something you don't regret doing. I know the difference between right and wrong and I know what I did to you was wrong, but I don't regret falling in love with you. I don't regret the nights we spent together and I won't regret what I'm about to do.

I love you, Raleigh. I love you more than you can possibly realize and, again, I know that it is unfair of me to tell you this. You should be moving on with your life, healing, finding a nice man who treats you well and who you will love for all the right reasons. But after everything I've done to you, I still have hope that you can learn to love me, learn to love all of me and not just because you need me, but because you want me.

The key which you are now holding in your hand unlocks my apartment in Paris. My parents left it to me and I want you to have it now. I'll be writing to you there from wherever it is they lock me away. I've called the landlord and told her your name, told her not to expect you but, in the event you do show up, to make sure you have everything you need. I robbed you once of the chance to escape your life and I don't want to do it again. Go to Paris, if not for me than for yourself. I don't know when I'll be free or if I'll ever see you again, but knowing that I was able to give you a chance to escape should get me through the days and nights where I don't get to see you or feel you by my side.

I'm going to hold on to the hope that one day I can see you again. I don't know when it will be and it's impossible to guess the circumstances, but I can tell you right now that moment will be the best moment of my life. I love you and I always will. You mean everything to me.

Kaden

Below his name was an address. I stared at the street number for a long moment before reading the letter again. My head struggled to accept everything that I had just read and everything I now knew. Kaden was in prison, serving a four year sentence for rape and kidnapping. But he loved me; he wanted me to be free and live my life; he wanted me to make the decisions that were right for me. Yet, my heart no longer felt whole. I felt as if I were missing some large piece of me, some piece that would change me to a we. I was a part of him now and he was undeniably a part of me. Much like I had been during those long weeks in captivity, Kaden now lacked the ability to make decisions for himself. It was now up to me to make the right choices for *us*.

How Kaden would fit into my life, I didn't know. Would he return from prison one day so we could pick right back up where we left off, spending days together in his room, making love for hours and hours? Or would we try to start over? Would he do things the right way, asking me out on a date, letting our relationship grow in a natural progression? Or would we just live with the memory of each other, knowing that our other half was out there in the world and living their life? I believed that if he knew I was happy, Kaden would leave me alone, content in the knowledge that I was safe and doing well.

I didn't know if Paris would answer my questions. I didn't know what I would find in Kaden's apartment but I knew that I had to go. Maybe not tomorrow, maybe not next week, but I knew that before long I would find myself standing outside Kaden's door. I stood up, found my purse, dug for my keys, and placed my newest key on the ring. It looked like it belonged there.

I folded the letter and placed it on my night stand. I knew I would read it hundreds of times over. I turned the off the lights and shut the door behind me. I walked downstairs with a new direction in life. It wasn't a long term decision, but one that would get me through the next couple of months or weeks, however long I could hold out.

Chapter 27

I felt for the key in my pocket and pulled it out. I had held it so many times over the past few months. I had made up my mind weeks ago to come to Paris in order to open my eyes to a different side of the man who I loved. This was his apartment, his former life, and now I stood outside the door, utterly afraid to go in. I knew he wouldn't be inside but I didn't know what else to expect. I could enter this apartment, go through his things, and realize I hadn't known him at all. What terrified me even more was the possibility that I could realize I had known him all too well. Being surrounded by his things, his possessions, his memories, I knew it would be torture for me, a constant reminder of what I couldn't have and what I shouldn't want.

I looked behind me at the winding staircase and for a split second considered running down them and throwing the key into the Seine. The cool marble of the ancient building calmed me, the breeze blowing my hair lightly around my face. Kaden's door was the only one on this floor. It was tall and black, made from thick wood no doubt painted to match the iron work on the stair's banister. How many times had he walked these stairs, opened this door and made his way inside? I knew it was nothing more than a vacation home now, but perhaps he lived here as a child. I closed my eyes and imagined a small boy skipping through the courtyard of the building, his black hair shining in the sun, his emerald eyes sparkling with excitement. I never thought of Kaden as being innocent, but I supposed we all were at some point.

My attention returned to the door. I fit the key into the lock and turned the handle. My future would be decided within the walls of this apartment, within the remnants of Kaden's life. I reveled in the fact that it would be mine to decide; it couldn't be taken from me. The door opened without much effort and I stepped over a large pile of white envelopes. I knew instantly that they were all for me. Gathering them in my hands, I placed them on a small table near a brilliant royal blue and gold vase. I ran my fingers down its smooth side before looking over the rest of the entry way. The ceilings were high and the walls were painted a bright yellow. A large, round mirror hung above the table and I smiled at my reflection. My blonde curls were longer than they had been in a while, my skin had a healthy shine, and my grey eyes looked alive.

I removed my coat and hung it on a peg, slipped out of my shoes and felt the smooth finish of the tiled floor beneath my toes. A long hallway was on my left and a small bathroom was on my right. I walked straight ahead and found myself in the kitchen. All the appliances looked vintage World War II but the granite countertops and bright red accents of the room gave it a modern feel. I opened cupboards and drawers, acquainting myself with everything. There was no food in the house, just mixing bowls, utensils, and the occasional canned item. I smiled when I found a can of tuna sitting next to some dried pasta.

Beyond the kitchen was the dining room, a dark room with chocolate walls and gold place settings. It looked undisturbed and very formal, perhaps only used for holidays and fancy dinner parties. A glass chandelier hung from the ceiling and the light from the one window on the far side of the room reflected around the crystals like a game of light tag. I knew that Kaden would only use this formal a room if forced to do so.

I turned back toward the foyer, opening the kitchen window on my way, and peered down the hallway. Pictures hung on the walls and I tiptoed to the first one. I recognized Kaden instantly. He was young, a boyish smile on his face as he stood in a small boat, proudly holding a fishing pole in one hand and a large catfish in the other. His bright orange life jacket nearly smothered him. I wondered if the picture had been taken at the same lake where we saw the blue heron.

The next photo was a family portrait. Kaden was absolutely his father's son. They shared the same strong features, the same dark hair and flawless skin, and the same smile. But he had his mother's eyes. Her light brown hair fell to her shoulders. She sat between her two men, her hands gently folded in her lap. She looked elegant and refined with a single strand of pearls around her neck. Her kind, green eyes sparkled with mischief and the crooked grin on her face let everyone know that she was in charge of this family.

I walked slowly down the hall, examining each and every photo: Kaden's high school graduation, family vacations, a wedding portrait of his mom and dad - each framed memory helped paint the picture of Kaden's past. I realized I really knew very little about this man. Is this what he enjoyed doing in his spare time? Fishing and traveling? I now had two versions of Kaden. The first was the man I loved, the one who had hurt me yet protected me, fought for me and gave up everything just so he could be with me. The second was a stranger. He looked like Kaden, but I knew nothing about him. I didn't know his life, I didn't know his dreams or ambitions. I wanted to believe that with time, these two men would become one but I knew I had so much more to learn.

The first door I came to turned out to be nothing more than a linen closet, towels and extra bedding folded neatly on the shelves. The next was a large bedroom with an ornate four post bed, the wood carved into various designs. The windows were closed and when I flipped the light switch, nothing happened. I crossed the hardwood floor and opened the shutters, warm sunlight instantly flooding the space. The bed and a small dresser were the only pieces of furniture in the room. The closet was open and empty and there were small holes in the walls where more pictures used to hang. This must have been a guest room or his parent's master bedroom. I opened the window to remove the dust from the sill and left the door open before returning to the hallway.

I came to a small parlor next. The walls were a delicate blue and the white furniture made the sitting room look clean and polished. I held my breath at the last door, knowing that it had to be Kaden's room. The handle stuck so I had to push to open the door. The walls were painted nearly the same shade of grey as his room back at the lake. There were no pictures or photographs. The green quilt on the bed was soft and I lifted one of the pillows. Pressing the soft down to my face, I inhaled deeply, hoping to smell remnants of him.

I clung to the pillow, smiling. Kaden's bookshelf was next. It reached to the ceiling and spanned nearly the entire wall. Hardbacks and leather bindings with French and English titles were arranged by what appeared to be genre, though I didn't recognize half of them; loose-leaf notebooks lay on the bottom shelf. I picked up the first one, what appeared to be the oldest, and flipped through the pages, the date at the top from ten years ago. Kaden's penmanship looked very much the same although not as neat as it had been in the letter he sent. The pages were filled with his lessons, all in French, which I couldn't read.

His closet was next and I opened the large doors, not at all surprised to find only a few items hanging inside. A cardboard box had been taped shut and shoved to one side and a few pairs of shoes were neatly lined up on the shelf just above my head.

I turned around and walked to the window, finally opening the shutters so the sun could spill in. Being in his room only made me miss him more. It was like he was a ghost and I could almost feel his presence watching me as I poked through his things. But I knew he was alive and well, most likely sitting in his prison cell, perhaps thinking about me. I didn't like to think about Kaden in prison but the alternative was to imagine him here with me and that pushed me a little too close to the edge of insanity. He was there in my dreams and beside me when I closed my eyes.

I placed the pillow back on the bed and stripped down to my underwear. I placed my jeans and sweater on the chair next to the window and grabbed one of Kaden's shirts from his closet, pulled it over my shoulders and fastened the middle buttons. I wandered to the foyer and picked up the stack of letters from the table, flipping through them on my way back to Kaden's room. They were all addressed to the Prideaux's apartment, attention: Current Resident. I recognized Kaden's handwriting and saw that the return address was thc North Carolina State Penitentiary.

Sitting on the bed, I spread the letters out in front of me. There were dozens of them and I gazed over the envelopes, trying to decide which one to open first. I ultimately decided that I should organize them by date and I squinted to read the small numbers printed on the seal. Opening the first letter, I couldn't even feel my hands ripping through the envelope. I unfolded the paper as if in a trance and smiled at my name written on the top of the page.

Dear Raleigh,

This is the first time I've been allowed to write to anyone. It's been almost three weeks since I last saw you and the pain has increased to an almost unbearable level. But I don't remember a time when my conscience has been so clear. I know that you are probably livid right now and you have every right to be angry at me. You know why I did it, though, and I hope that one day you can forgive me.

My days are spent sitting in my cell and thinking about you, thinking about our time together. I often have to remind myself that I am at fault because it's so easy to blame everyone else. Sometimes I blame you for being so beautiful, for being on the side of the road that night, for not fighting me off when you should have. More often than not, I blame Ray for being so drunk, for scaring you so badly that you sought comfort from me, probably the worst person for the job of protector. Rarely do I blame Marshal for being weak and not standing up to me or his brother. But I've made my confession and won't recant it. I'm eager to plead guilty in front of a judge so that I can begin my sentence. I don't know how long it is going to be, but it will be a welcome relief when I can point to a date on a calendar and know that is the day I can be free again.

I'm not sure what else to say. I'm not even sure why I wrote this letter. Everything is still so up in the air - in transition - and I can't even think clearly. But writing to you, even though I know there is only a small possibility you will ever read it, reminds me that I have something to anchor to, something that will keep me sane.

I love you.

You are my everything.

Kaden

My hands flew to the next letter and I tore into it, ripping the paper from the envelope.

Dear Raleigh,

I was sentenced today. My lawyer struck a deal with the judge and I plead guilty to rape and kidnapping. Does it hurt to see those words written on paper? I almost couldn't write them because I've started to forget all of the bad things that happened and only choose to remember the good. I can't help but wonder which parts you are remembering, if any. Maybe you've pushed the entire time from your mind as a defense against the pain I caused you. I suppose I would deserve that just as much as I deserve my four year sentence. It should have been seven years but the lesser time is contingent on my testimony during Ray's trial. I'm not expected to lie or embellish, they just want me to take the witness stand. They say that if I do a good job, I'll be eligible for parole after 24 months. I didn't ask what would qualify as a good job because I only want to tell the truth, with no hidden agenda.

It's hard to believe that in a few months I'll be testifying against my best friend. I know that Marshal has been asked to do the same thing and I've encouraged him to go ahead and do it. Is it wrong to persuade him to stand against his brother? I don't think it is. Ray is no longer the same person he once was.

I'm trying to prevent myself from hoping that that you will be at the trial. I'm trying to convince myself that you will give your testimony and then leave for Delaware without sticking around to hear the verdict. I'll only be there to give my testimony. I may not even hear about the outcome for days after the trial has ended. I don't know if you've found the key I left in your bag. You may have thrown everything away, but if you haven't and if you read this before the trial, please know that everything I say up on that stand is going to be the truth. There's a lot that I didn't tell you about. I know you are very perceptive, but there are some things which I would rather keep hidden from you, some things which might scare you to this day. So hold on to whoever is there with you, know that you are safe and that I love you and that everything I do, every thought in my head is for you.

I love you.

You are my everything.

Kaden

I waded through the envelopes until I found one that had been dated just after the trial. My eyes were dry because I hadn't blinked and my head spun with emotions I couldn't even begin to organize. Twenty four months? In less than two years he could be out. I didn't know how I wanted to feel about that. It scared me to imagine that I could run into him out of the blue, once I had put my life back together. It excited me to think that I could be with him, back in his arms in less time that it took to for me to obtain a graduate degree.

Dear Raleigh,

God, how I miss you. Seeing you today was the greatest gift I could have received but also the greatest pain I've ever felt. You look exactly how I thought you would though I'm happy to see that you are still wearing your hair in curls. You are still every bit the girl I fell in love with, the girl I love to this day. I could tell from the second I saw you that you hadn't found my key and letter, which doesn't surprise me. I hope you picked up on my hint; I could see the wheels in your head turning.

The pain and confusion on your face when I spoke about the last night we spent together nearly broke me, Blondie. I didn't tell you about it at the time because I didn't want to scare you. I thought I was going to lose you that night. The look in Ray's eyes didn't leave a doubt in my mind that he was capable of shooting you. He asked if I had any last words to say to you and so I reached for your face and told you that I loved you. What it was about that statement that made him change his mind, I will never know. But he left and I screamed at the top of my lungs because I knew what I would have to do. I knew that turning myself in would be difficult, leaving you would be nearly impossible. But I'm hopeful now. You've given me hope.

Can you imagine what it would be like if we were still together? If we were on the run, completely lost to those who once knew us? I don't know how long it would have lasted. I'd like to think that you wouldn't grow sick of me and my endless need to protect you from everything. You'd yell at me constantly and I'd yell back because I wouldn't know what else to do. Then one day you would leave me. But I think you would keep our secret. I don't think you would turn me in.

Until I saw you today, I hadn't allowed myself to think about what could happen four years from now. I know that I should leave you be; I know that I shouldn't hope for a reunion of any kind. You're well aware that what we had together wasn't in your best interests and I certainly don't deserve a second chance. But the look on your face when I was leaving the courtroom said it all. I know that I've created demons for you, demons which you now have to live with on a daily basis because you know that loving me is wrong. But it won't always be, I promise you that. I promise that I will live the rest of my life trying to be the person you deserve, regardless of if I ever get to see you again.

I love you, Raleigh. I love you so much and just knowing that you love even a small part of me - the wrong side of me - is worth my wait here in prison.

You are and will always be my everything.

Kaden

I spent the rest of the afternoon going through each and every letter. I cried when he spoke of how much he missed me, how he thought about me constantly, how he tortured himself by remembering the horrible things he had done to me. But I smiled when he talked about how he dreamt of me, how whenever he closed his eyes, I was there by his side.

He spoke often about his life in prison; how he had become used to the routine, how he had made friends with some of the other inmates. He was teaching his cellmate how to speak French. In some letters he would just tell me stories about his childhood, his years at college. He claimed that these memories, which had seemed so insignificant, were now his most prized possessions. Some of the men inside had nothing but horrible pasts filled with hate and crime. But Kaden had been happy once and he had me and his memories to get him through the days.

My stomach was rumbling by the time I put down the last of his letters. The sun began to set over Paris and I stood up to get dressed. I wandered through the streets until I found a small market where I bought some groceries. I didn't know how long I would be staying here. It could be days. It could be months. I might never leave.

I felt more confident walking into the apartment for a second time, a paper bag under my arm. I prepared and ate my dinner without rush or ceremony, mostly trying to adjust to my life in Kaden's apartment.

When I was done, I knew it was time to reach out to him. He had been writing me for months and months, nearly a year, and had received nothing in return. His hopes and spirits were still high, that much I could tell. What would happen to him if he received a letter from me? Would it break him? Would it only encourage him further?

And the better question was what would happen to me if I wrote to him? It seemed obvious that I could depend on a letter from Kaden almost every week at the rate he had been writing. That was enough to get me through the days until I decided what I wanted, wasn't it? No, I wasn't fooling myself this time. I knew that I would write to him, I had to write to him. I had so many questions to ask, so much to say. I deserved answers.

I walked back to his room and picked up one of the notebooks, flipping to the back pages and finding a blank one. I crawled back into his bed, ready to compose. I wasn't going to commit to anything permanent, wasn't going to make promises I wasn't ready to keep.

Dear Kaden,

I arrived at your apartment earlier today. It's nothing like what I expected but I guess I didn't really have a strong idea of what I would find. And I've read all your letters. Again, not really what I expected but they seemed to be exactly what I needed.

The feeling of not knowing you is strange to me. I remember you and think about you as one person, but then I come here and my entire perception has changed. You had a life before me, a happy, wonderful life and I don't really understand why you allowed yourself to throw all that away. You'll probably tell me it's because I was worth it but I won't believe you – or I don't want to believe you. No one has loved me like you have. We have a strange and unconventional love and I am still struggling to understand it. It's funny how something so scary and foreign can grow to feel so amazing. Thinking about you, loving you the way that I do, it used to be terrifying but now it's almost liberating in a way. Does that make any sense?

I wish there was some way of seeing the future. These two or three years are going to pass quickly yet so much is going to happen. I'm not putting my life on hold for you, Kaden. I refuse to do that and I can't imagine you would want me to. I may learn to live without you. I may decide that is what is best for me. Or not. I might decide I need some part of you, need all of you. I suppose only time will tell and time is exactly what we have.

Do you remember when time was working against us? When you said that our time together was limited? I needed you so desperately then. You protected me and gave me reason to hope, showed me that I was still human. I hated myself for giving you that dominance but at the end of the day, I know that it was what I needed. Just as you needed to turn yourself in to save me, I needed to fall for you in order to save myself. I believe I would have withered away and died in that basement had it not been for you.

And I do blame you for ruining what we had. I had been prepared to run away with you, to start over and to trust you. But you took that from me. I was angry and hurt by what you did to me, to us. But what you did for Julie and what you did for Carla, that makes up for it. I'm still alive and breathing; they are not.

I suppose, in a way, what you did gave me a choice. I could feel it happening, you know? I could feel myself start to heal and I knew that with only a little persuasion, I could push you from my heart entirely. I doubt you will ever be pushed from my mind but I'm convinced I could learn not to love you. But, Kaden, I do want to believe that you are a person I should love, that somewhere inside of you there is a person who deserves me. Please don't believe that I want you to prove anything to me. I want to find it for myself and I'm not ashamed to say that I will be searching for it.

I don't know how long I will stay in Paris. I love this city and staying in the apartment where you used to live will make it terribly hard for me to leave. I'll be waiting for your letters and most likely re-reading all of the old ones until the pages have fallen apart. I don't want some declaration of love in your next letter. I don't want more confessions of guilt. I just want you to be you and write from your heart. Write for yourself and not for me because I have everything I need right here in your apartment.

I love you, Kaden. Against my better judgment and sense, I love you and I'm making the conscious decision to keep loving you until the day I die. But for right now, please keep sending me letters and we'll figure this out together. I have hope for us.

You have my heart,
Raleigh

Epilogue

I smiled at Matthieu. He smiled back, his slightly wrinkled lips exposing false teeth. In my two and a half years in Paris, Matthieu had become my closest friend. I had never imagined that as my 30th birthday approached, I would be living in a foreign country and spending the majority of my time with a 75 year old grandfather with whom I could barely communicate. Granted, we understood more of each other now than when we had first met, but we still shared those frustrating moments when neither of us could say or sign the things we really meant.

I had met Matthieu and his oldest son during my first week in Paris. They had a small business selling homemade pasta and I had happened upon their stall while I was wandering the market looking for groceries. Paul-Henri had seen me studying the different pastas and eagerly tried to make a sale, speaking in French while all I could do was stare at him. Luckily, Matthieu had intervened and asked me something which looked like it could have been in English.

"English?" I had asked quietly. "I'm sorry, I don't speak French."

It took them both a long moment to realize my unique situation, and while Paul-Henri looked flabbergasted by the challenge, Matthieu gave me a bright smile and pulled a pencil out of his pocket.

"Would you like to buy some pasta?" he wrote and I eagerly nodded my head.

And for a few weeks, that is how we communicated. We would write and point and nod or shake our heads. It wasn't much, but it was the only personal interaction I had with anyone apart from the emails to my father and my friends back home. It was nice to use my voice, even if only for a few minutes each day.

Then one day Paul-Henri asked how long I would be staying in France. I had told him that my plans were uncertain, but as of that day, I would be staying indefinitely. He smiled and then said something to his father who nodded in return. After that, things were written in English and French, and thus my lessons began.

I never got around to telling Matthieu why I was in France. He had asked once and I said I was staying at a friend's apartment while he was out of town. As the weeks turned into months, and then into years, we never discussed the subject again, which is why I was surprised when he brought it up so suddenly.

"Cherie." Matthieu addressed me with the same term of endearment he used with his daughters and granddaughters. I truly believed I had become part of his family. "Why are you still in Paris? Has your friend never come home to claim his apartment?" He repeated his questions in French and I watched carefully as his lips moved, picking up a word every so often.

"No. He hasn't come home," I said, hoping he couldn't see the conflict which raged behind my eyes. The last letter I had received from Kaden had been nearly 5 months ago. He had written and said he was up for parole and that he was hoping to see me soon. He would be waiting for my letter, the letter I was supposed to write letting him know if I wanted him to come to France or if I wanted him to stay away.

I never wrote back.

I couldn't write back. What was I supposed to say to that? Prison allowed me to go on without having to make a decision about our relationship. He had to be there. He couldn't leave and so it was easy for me to keep up the correspondence with him, knowing that no matter what I said or what feelings I confessed, there was an entire ocean and many steel bars between us. The illusion of Kaden, the man who claimed to love me and dream about me every night, had quickly replaced the monster everyone assumed he was. But I knew that if I saw him, if I felt him touch me, that illusion would be shattered. And I simply wasn't ready to let it go.

It was difficult, not writing to Kaden. I had looked forward to his letters, which arrived every Thursday and continued to arrive even though I stopped writing back. I hadn't opened one since. I didn't want to know what he had to say. I didn't want him to convince me that we should start over, that I should give him a second chance, just like I didn't want him to tell me he wasn't coming. Why should I have to make this decision? I was the one who had been hurt.

"But you will stay in France, won't you?" Matthieu asked.

"Of course I will. It's my home now," I answered with a smile.

"It makes me happy to hear you say that."

We grinned at each other and I finished my coffee. It had been a boring day at work but French lessons with Matthieu had brightened my mood. My father had supplemented my income for nearly 6 months after I left, clearly believing that I was on an extended vacation. It broke his heart when I asked him if he knew anyone at the US Embassy who could get me a job and a permanent work visa, but he pulled some strings and I started a job as a part time filing clerk. At least at the Embassy I could understand what people were saying, though the conversation was never very interesting. Nevertheless, I made a few friends. Between Matthieu and 'the Americans' as he called them, I found myself feeling more and more comfortable in my new surroundings.

"I need to pick up some things before I go home," I said in French. Matthieu flashed a big smile although I could tell he had struggled to understand what I was trying to say.

"Very well, Ma Cherie. À demain."

"Until tomorrow," I repeated and stood up to leave.

Matthieu walked me to the door of his small flat and kissed both my cheeks.

I left my friend's apartment feeling uncertain, a mood which had been virtually unknown to me for some time now. Maybe not completely unknown, but certainly suppressed.

My uneasiness stayed with me for nearly two weeks after I left Matthieu's apartment and grew stronger with each passing day. It felt like my mind was counting down to something, some great surprise or culminating finale. I couldn't stand the feeling, but there was little I could do. So I made my way silently through the streets of Paris, going about my daily routine as best I could.

And then one day, the countdown ended, just like I had hoped and dreaded it would.

* * *

I made my way silently through the busy Paris streets, ducking into the grocery store near my apartment just as it started to rain. I took my time gathering the things I needed, meandering up and down the aisles and trying to kick the trepidation I felt. Maybe I should read Kaden's letters. At least I would know his plans. Maybe he had decided on his own that he wasn't going to come see me. Would they even let him out of the country if he were on parole? Surely one of my friends or my father would have warned me if he had been released. But then again, they had their own lives to lead and I had adamantly campaigned for everyone to leave the trial and my kidnapping in the past. Maybe they had done that, or maybe they just wanted to make me think they had.

The rain hadn't stopped once my groceries had been paid for and the streets were visibly less crowded. With a bag under each arm, I walked as quickly as I could to the apartment and let myself into the courtyard. The marble stairs were slick with rainwater and I took my time, carefully watching my steps as I made my way up to the now familiar black door of Kaden's apartment.

Looking just a few stairs ahead of me, I stopped as I came around the last corner. A pair of grey sneakers rested just in my line of vision. Attached were two denim clad legs, bending at the knee. Their owner sat on the landing. He must have heard me climbing the stairs because he was sitting up straight, his hands neatly folded

in his lap. But he couldn't have known that it was me.
Maybe he just hoped it would be.

Kaden's face was exactly how it should be - no longer
tired and worn like in the courtroom, but strong and fierce
like it had been the night he had kidnapped me. What
seemed like millions of memories flashed before my eyes -
the trunk of the car, Julie's body, Kaden's touch, Ray's
glare, Marshal's innocence. Neither of us moved as I
studied his expression, wondering if I should be terrified,
relieved, or overjoyed. His jaw clenched as he tried to
keep his emotions at bay, but his emerald eyes betrayed
his calm. He was scared. I had never seen this part of him
before. On the witness stand, even on the day he turned
himself in, he was never scared. Wary, sure. Uncertain,
only at times. But scared? I didn't even know he was
capable of feeling that way.

The bags in my arms suddenly felt unbearably heavy.
My muscles started to quiver as I waited for him to speak.
But we remained there in silence. I could feel the water
dripping from my hair onto my neck and face. My skirt
must have been clinging to my legs but I couldn't bring
myself to move.

Suddenly Kaden jumped and I let out a gasp, terrified
he was going to attack. A look of sadness crossed his face
as he slowly stood up.

"Thunder," he explained in one word and I knitted my brow in confusion.

Thunder? That was the first thing he could think to say to me after all this time?

"I didn't mean to startle you," he continued. He took a step toward me and I held my breath. "Can I carry those for you?"

I nodded slowly, holding out one bag and then the other. Kaden took them, careful not to let our hands touch, and then turned to walk up the remaining stairs to his apartment. I waited until he was at the door before following him, my legs barely moving as I did so. It felt all too surreal, unlocking the door as Kaden waited patiently. He kept his distance, which I was grateful for, and watched me intently as I stepped out of my shoes and left them under the table in the entryway. I took the groceries from him so he could do the same and immediately walked to the kitchen.

I put the groceries away, trying to convince myself that nothing about this evening was different. That nothing had really changed. But when I was done, I had no choice but to turn toward the door and see Kaden standing there. A small smile graced his lips.

"I see you've made yourself at home," he said.

"Yes," I replied, my voice scratchy in my throat. "Oui."

His smile widened and I could see his fear dissipating. "And you've learned French?"

"Juste un peu," I confessed. Only a little.

He took a large step toward me and raised his hand as if he were reaching for me. "Raleigh, I..."

"Stop!" I said forcefully and he became as still as a statue. "Please don't come any closer."

"Okay," he nodded in understanding and composed his thoughts before speaking again. "I can see from your face that you didn't know I was coming. I wrote to let you know that I would be here, but I hadn't heard from you in so long..." he didn't finish his thought because we both knew that I hadn't been writing. "I didn't even know if I would still find you here."

"When did they let you out?"

He raised his eyebrows, probably realizing that I hadn't been reading any of his letters. "Almost five months ago."

"And they let you leave the country?"

"I had to renounce my US citizenship. I've done a lot of jumping through hoops to get here. That's why it's taken me so long to get to you," he added slowly.

I nodded but then shook my head. "And what if I hadn't been here?"

"I would have found a way back to you." His confidence was back and I didn't doubt for a second what he said.

"Have you talked to Marshal?" I asked suddenly, wanting to remain in control of the conversation. Looking at Kaden, speaking to Kaden, hell, even thinking about Kaden caused an avalanche of memories to fall directly on my head, the good mixed in with the bad. But thinking about Marshal was different. I had no negative memories associated with him. I would always think of him as my knight in shining armor.

Kaden, winced upon hearing his name. It probably brought too many bad memories back. "I saw him once, a few weeks after I got out. He's working on a fishing boat a few towns down from..." He paused to clear his throat. I could see his entire body, from his brow to his knees, was tense. "...from my house."

His house. The one where I had been held captive for so many weeks: starved, raped and beaten. The house where I fell in love with Kaden.

"How is he?" Marshal had never deserved his prison sentence, in my opinion. He had gotten 24 months. He had walked out after 18. Three weeks before his release, Ray had been stabbed during a fight. He had died in prison before his case made it through the first appeal.

Kaden had written to tell me what had happened, but I felt absolutely nothing. No relief, no sadness, no joy. Nothing. Neither of us had ever spoken of Ray again.

"He seems to be doing well," Kaden answered, and I smiled. "After his parole, he says he's going to move to Alaska to work on fishing boats up there. I guess he likes it well enough."

"I'm happy for him."

"He asked if I was going to find you," Kaden said quickly, looking rather ashamed.

"What did you tell him?"

"I didn't lie." Kaden looked at me as though he were seeking my approval. "He told me I should stay away, let you get on with your life."

I raised my eyebrows and waited to hear his excuse.

Kaden's face sank. Maybe he wanted me to tell him that I was glad he showed up today. That wasn't going to happen. Not just yet.

"I told him that I would stay away if that's what you wanted. But I needed to hear it from you first."

I merely nodded in understanding.

"He said he was happy to see me," Kaden continued, "but he didn't want me dropping by again."

I swallowed the lump in my throat. Marshal, innocent and kind Marshal, had been tainted by Ray and Kaden. I hoped he could put his life back together.

I didn't know what else to say so I stood there, waiting for him to make the next move.

"Why did you stop writing Raleigh?" he asked. Was he now the one who was desperate for answers? I had been there once; I knew how helpless he must have felt.

"You were asking too much," I told him, knowing I was going to have to explain myself. "You wanted me to send you an answer; you wanted me to make a decision and I couldn't do it. I shouldn't want you here, and part of me truly doesn't." I couldn't prevent the tears from falling from my eyes. "But now that you are here, standing in front of me and I can actually see you talking to me and see that you aren't just living in my imagination, I feel like I have found a part of me that has been missing."

So much had been said between us during his time in prison. I held nothing back in my letters, never once sparing his feelings. I hadn't let him forget why he was there, what he had done to deserve this punishment. There were times when I felt disgusted with myself for allowing our relationship to continue. The letters were raw, intimate, and honest despite the distance between us. There were times when I missed him more than anything. And there were times when I hated him. I wrote him all of this and he took it in stride. Never once did Kaden deny his guilt but never once did he apologize. He had done that before, the last night we were together, and I still felt as if he meant every word of it. I didn't need to hear it again.

"If you want me to leave, I'll leave. I just need to hear you say it," Kaden said. "But nothing would make me happier than for you to ask me to stay."

And there it was again. The choice was up to me and I, in no way, wanted to make that decision.

"You never gave me a choice before," I said coldly. He flinched. I knew that would hurt him. "So you'll have to excuse me if I hesitate."

"I'm not asking you to make up your mind completely. Just for tonight. Do you want me to stay or do you want me to leave?"

I sighed and went with my first instinct. "Leave."

He nodded his head. "I'll see you tomorrow."

He turned toward the door before I could read his expression and I instinctively took two steps after him.

"Kaden, wait."

He looked over his shoulder at me before turning his body. "I nearly forgot what it sounded like when you said my name," he said.

I wanted to speak but I couldn't. The memory of the first time I had spoken his name hit me like a slap in the face. Kaden had been an entirely different person to me at that time: a mystery, a monster, a glimmer of hope in a terrifying nightmare. But that wasn't the man I saw in front of me now. The emotions I had once felt in his presence, the horror, the uncertainty, the anguish, they were quickly dissipating as I realized that I was now in control. I didn't have to relinquish anything to Kaden if I didn't want to.

"Knowing that you are here, I don't think I'll be able to sleep tonight if you leave."

"Then I'll stay," he said, taking a hesitant step in my direction. We were now close enough to touch and I could feel my fingers itching to reach for him. He must have been feeling the same way because he slowly lifted his hand. He hesitated before touching my face but when I didn't shy away, he gently brushed a stray curl from my cheek.

"I've missed you so much, Blondie."

I smiled for the first time since seeing him. He smiled back and his fingers stroked my skin. I closed my eyes, savoring his touch, but quickly opened them when I remembered how little I trusted him.

"I'm not going to hurt you," he promised, reading me as he always had. "Never again will I hurt you."

I nodded and closed my eyes, giving in and letting him hold me. His arms encased me like a warm blanket on a cold night as he held me close to his chest. I felt as though I was floating, liberated from some prison I had been keeping myself in. His body this close to mine didn't scare me, as I thought it would. It felt familiar and safe and I never wanted him to let me go.

Had I created a new illusion for myself? Now that Kaden was here, had I somehow convinced my mind to forget all the horrible things he had done to me? To Julie and to Carla? No. I certainly still remembered being kept in the basement, being denied food, being forced into submission. But I had somehow come to terms with it. I remembered what Kaden had said at the lake. He wasn't a bad person; he had just made some fucked up decisions. I wasn't a bad person either, but by many standards, I had made some really fucked up decisions. Leaving my friends and family to live in Kaden's apartment in Paris? Kaden, the man who had kidnapped and raped me. Not that my decisions hurt anyone but myself. Certainly they would confuse people, but no one was physically or emotionally damaged by them.

Kaden held me for what seemed like hours. Hundreds of emotions ran through my mind but only one kept returning - relief. Relief that he was here, relief that I had stayed strong, relief that he still wanted me, and relief that I knew we could make it through. Kaden had my heart even after all of our time apart, even after I gave up needing him, even after I had learned to hate him.

I finally felt him pull away and I opened my eyes to look up at him. I could see that he felt relieved as well. He no longer looked scared but his eyes stared at me with sadness and longing. His hand lifted from my shoulder so he could sign.

I love you.

I looked at his hand and knew it to be true. Gently, I raised mine and placed my fingers lightly on the front of his neck.

"I want to feel you say it," I told him.

"I love you," he said without reservation and I smiled as I reached for his hand and placed it over my heart.

"I love you too."

The warmth from his smile filled the room and I took comfort in knowing that I had caused him such happiness.

"Now prove to me that you deserve it," I challenged him and he chuckled.

"Where do you want me to start?"

"Dinner would be nice."

Kaden smiled and looked as if he were about to kiss me. His eyes glanced down at my lips but he took a step back once he realized I had figured out what he was thinking.

"I need to earn that too, don't I?" He asked with a grin.

I smiled before taking a seat at the kitchen table. Watching Kaden work his way around the kitchen was like watching a child rediscover a favorite toy. Kaden had once loved this place and probably still did. I hadn't moved anything, but memories aren't always as accurate as one would like them to be. He slowly opened and examined every drawer and cupboard as if finding a small memory of his childhood in each piece of kitchenware.

We made small talk over dinner. He asked me about what I did from day to day even though he already knew. He was happy that I liked Paris, that I considered it my home. He didn't ask about my family or friends, if they missed me or if they wanted me to return to Delaware. Those questions, just like the questions I had about prison, would wait for a later time. But everything would eventually be laid out on the table. All skeletons would come out of the closet and all fears would be addressed. It would happen one day at a time.

* * *

As I slowly let Kaden back into my physical world, I grew to appreciate how much he had meant to my emotional one. I had been running away from everything and everyone I had known when I met Kaden. The time I spent with him had turned my worst nightmare into a reality, but it had taught me so much about the human heart. I could never justify my feelings for Kaden to anyone and I had learned to control my own expectations and not allow others to dictate them. So it didn't surprise me when one day I found myself leading Kaden down the hallway to the bedroom. Not one step of this process had been easy for either of us and I knew that giving Kaden my body would be one of the most difficult things I had ever done. But we were ready.

I closed my eyes as Kaden kissed me and lifted me onto the bed. I tried not to anticipate the fear or regret I might feel while making love. As I felt the smooth sheets beneath my back and Kaden's body above me, I started to panic. I opened my eyes and Kaden looked at me with a mixture of sadness and the guilt, determination and kindness.

"We don't have to do this," he said and I could tell he was whispering.

"I want to," I told him. "But it's been so long and I'm afraid."

"Afraid of me?"

"Yes. And afraid of everything this implies."

Kaden lifted one of my hands which had been clenching the sheets, kissing each finger before setting it gently by my side. "Do you remember the last time we were together?"

I nodded.

"I asked you to close your eyes and imagine you were anywhere but in my bedroom with me."

I nodded again.

"Try it again. Close your eyes and try to think if you would rather be anywhere else in the entire world. And, if you find a place, we'll get up right now and go there."

I took a deep breath. Slowly, my eyes closed and I willed my body to relax. I could still feel Kaden on the bed next to me. He was drawing circles on my hip with his fingers and gently kissing my neck and shoulder. I tried to think of some exotic or distant location I had seen in a magazine or read about. Bali, Bangladesh, Belize. I'd love to see the entire world. But I was in no hurry.

I thought of my friends back in Delaware, how they were living their lives without me and how much I missed them. But even the longing I had for my friends couldn't replace the happiness I felt in Paris. With Kaden.

I started to shake my head as I opened my eyes. "No," I whispered, a tear running down my face. "I don't want to be anywhere else."

Kaden nodded his head and kissed each of my eyelids. I felt all hesitation and regret melt away. I knew that I had become officially liberated from every rope and chain that Kaden had ever tied to me. I didn't need him; he wasn't taking anything from me. I simply wanted him.

We made love all afternoon. Like everything in our new relationship, all it took was time for us to find our stride again.

* * *

And now, with a child on the way, and years of hard work and happiness to make up for the weeks of pain and sadness, I have never once regretted asking Kaden to stay that night.

THE END

Lydia Kelly grew up in Portland, Oregon where she lives with her husband. She attributes much of her creative inspiration to her friends and family who have always supported her every venture. *Screaming in the Silence* is her first novel and she is currently working on a series of young adults books.

Lydia Kelly's second book, *A Harper's Education*, is available online from all major booksellers.

CPSIA information can be obtained at www.ICGtesting.com
Printed in the USA
LVOW13s2016090813

347194LV00029B/693/P